THE LONELY BARBER

ANTHONY LABRIOLA

ANAPHORA LITERARY PRESS

BROWNSVILLE, TEXAS

ANAPHORA LITERARY PRESS
1898 Athens Street
Brownsville, TX 78520
http://anaphoraliterary.com

Book design by Anna Faktorovich, Ph.D.

Cover Image Based on: "Fresco from Vienna Opera House Representing scene from the *Barber of Seville.*" *Famous Composers and Their Works.* (1906). John Knowles Paine; Theodore Thomas; Karl Klauser, eds. Wikimedia Commons.

Published in 2017 by Anaphora Literary Press

The Lonely Barber
Anthony Labriola—1st edition.

Library of Congress Control Number: 2016962179

Library Cataloging Information
Labriola, Anthony, 1950-, author.
The Lonely Barber / Anthony Labriola
140 p. ; 9 in.
ISBN 978-1-68114-302-6 (softcover : alk. paper)
ISBN 978-1-68114-303-3 (hardcover : alk. paper)
ISBN 978-1-68114-304-0 (e-book)
1. Fiction—Romance—Contemporary. 2. Fiction—Urban Life.
3. Fiction—Literary. I. Title.
PS 8001-8599: Canadian Literature.
800 Literature & Rhetoric

THE LONELY BARBER

ANTHONY LABRIOLA

Dedication

To Nic, Sam and Lucy, in love and work—

I dedicate this tale with love as a somewhat irreverent and belated wedding gift, an urban legend, in honour of their coming together, despite the odds, and staying strong in pursuit of their dream, an inspiration to us all to endure and prevail.

we be sound to beat to bass to bone to flesh
we be sound to beat to bass to bone to flesh
we are truly miraculous
—Mayda del Valle

Before the real city could be seen it had to be imagined, the way rumours and tall tales were a kind of charting.
—Michael Ondaatje, *In the Skin of the Lion*

Ahimè, che folla! Uno alla volta, per carità!
Ehi, Figaro!
Son qua.
Figaro qua, Figaro là, Figaro su, Figaro giù.
—From *The Barber of Seville* by Giachino Rossini, with lyrics by Cesare Sterbini

PART ONE

1. The Straight Razor

Electric blue sparks spit into the ozone. They shoot, load and shock the air with a positive charge. The intersection at College and Spadina grounds the negative. The streetcar's trolley pole disconnects from the overhead cable. While the conductor is getting it back on the wire, with traffic at a standstill, the incident *nearly* happens. How does it get there so fast: v-i-o-l-e-n-c-e? Why does the victim always have to know? A guy his ex has nicknamed Lonely is seeking his *bliss* in the city. Now *this*. In the blitz of a ballistic breakup, "Bliss, my ass" is what she keeps saying at the Café where she works. Does anybody listen to a waitress's bellyache over the noise of café life complaints and lamentations, besides the cook?

"It's *lousy* to be jealous," he shouts over the clatter, clash and crash of plates and cutlery. "Jealousy is jea*lousy*. Best to pluck the stingers out of your three B's. *Bliss, blitz and breakup*: that's all your jealous ass ever talks about. And, *jeals*, just look what it's done to you."

No longer dealing with her three B's or jealous ass, Lonely is staring hard out the window, as if looking for a thrill-kill in the Six. He runs his long, thin fingers up the sides of his face, up the sideburns, and up through masses of curly fair amber blond hair, shaped upwards. He resembles a young Tom Waits. Two unidentified mockers in a black Hummer start staring him down, eyes locked in a violent embrace, blocked in a traffic jam. Since they are mocking him, Lonely offers them a middle finger apiece. The more he stares them down, the more they mock. It's a provocation, and Lonely feels provoked. More and more, he has been feeling that way in the city.

"Right, right," says Lonely.

Laughter and tears usually come to the same thing in the end. Lonely lifts himself out of his seat and motions for them to meet him at the next stop. He is up for a street brawl, the way it used to be in the city. That is, before the *Gentrification of Toronto*, the *Occupy Movement*, *Nudes on Bikes*, *Movember* and *Hipster Moustaches* make a street fight seem like an urban joke.

"All jokes are real in the city," Lonely says to the glare. "Am I fucking right?"

Or they become urban legends, like the story of the Lonely Barber. When it happens, it happens quickly as a kind of communal storytelling, a collective fable, or city-born lie, rumour or fiction. Even the agreed-upon version (even fictionalized) often includes the perversion of facts. Who gets to tell your story anyway? Tongues wag in Toronto's neighbourhoods, districts, and villages in a city built in a forest. So what else can anyone expect from long-tongued liars before they're cut down, but the telling of tall tales? Who will tell the story? And how will it be told? They tell it the only way they know how: their way. Still, life-writers keep writing, but do they ever get life right? Everybody is implicated, reliable or unreliable, but is *truth* ever on their side?

Beyond the stare down, the black Hummer's shadowy driver sticks the middle finger of his own right hand into his twisted mouth, sucks on it, withdraws it prematurely, and holds it up to the windshield. Lonely has his Pearl Straight Razor in his pant's pocket and will give him a close shave, and, contrary to his code and barbering skills, draw blood. But the trolley pole snaps back on the cicada-singing wire. The streetcar is belling and starting. Traffic lights change. All vehicles clear the corner. The mocking black Hummer speeds through the unclogged intersection. Threat levels rise to *high alert*. Speed loads the air with the scorching, electrical smell of v-i-o-l-e-n-c-e.

Lonely has to let it go and pay the beating forward. That leads to another *beating*, a woman he isn't sure of. It's 1 p.m. Lonely is late. He can just hear his abandoned lover booing him with:

"Let's all bleed for him, yeah right."

"It sucks to be jealous, especially over the likes of *him*," the cook raps, handing her a plate of pasta and clams. "Jealousy is like biting into your own face, chewing and swallowing yourself whole."

Lonely has a *late* lunch date with Simone Rebello. And, if she is *down*, and all women have to be down for him, at that defining moment of his life, he will let her in on his scheme, plan or vision, depending on the intimacy. Just as he has done with *The Waitress*, as he calls her. That is, before he dumps her, or thinks he does for good, not once but twice. Everybody is talking about it in dark whispers, and its shockwave will likely hit and burst the wrong eardrums. Wrong in the sense that the last ones to hear about it are usually family, but the first to strike back. Then jealousy trades places with revenge.

All that Simone Rebello likely knows about him is that his nickname is Lonely. He is trying to keep it *stupid* simple: to set up a retro barbershop called *The Lonely Barber* on Clinton Street south of College in Little Italy. If it does well, a *one-barber* barbershop with one barber chair, maybe two, he will put a sign in the window saying: *Lonely No More.* The chair is already there: a Pibbs Antigua Old Fashioned Old World Porcelain Italian Barber Chair with Red Leather.

"All right, it's a *reproduction* Old Italian style chair with an adjustable headrest," he says to older barbers that listen or half-listen to him with downcast eyes and stone faces. "The chair is made from solid steel and porcelain with a thick cushion in red."

Lonely loves the reclining backrest with kick-out old-fashioned frame.

"The real deal, manufactured in Italy," Lonely says to Sam, a College Street barber, "and made to last, as nearly as I can tell."

"But who cares about the chair?" Sam says as if giving him advice on the business. "You're there to cut hair and collect the cash. Money *talks* and bullshit *walks*."

On the two-toned wall of *The Lonely Barber*: an enormous ornate mirror, framed with walnut. On the makeshift counter: a Gaggia Classic espresso maker and tiny cups. If you get a haircut, you get an espresso. The cut costs you, but the *glory* is free. The shampoo station is the small washroom at the back of the shop. The sign in navy blue and vanilla is already up. The logo features the name with a flat, fat, vertical comb: *The Lonely Barber*. Identical blue benches are fitted: one inside, one outside. Lonely carves and paints his own barber pole in red and white. He mounts it with fasteners direct to chipped and crumbling red brick at the corner of the building. He plans to open when he gets approval from City Hall. But City Hall is protected by the bronze *Archer.*[1] It can defend your civic rights or pierce you through your heart with bronze-tipped arrows. Lonely's application is in. An inspector has already passed him. The inspection permit is on display in the arched window. But there is more to it than passing a sanitation inspection, right?

---

1   "The Archer" is a sculpture in front of the Toronto City Hall. *Three-Way Piece No. 2*, also known as "The Archer," unveiled in 1966, was originally created by Henry Moore, British, (1898-1986).

A Portuguese dude from the area bounces in one day, asking what the hell he is doing. When Lonely tells him he is setting up a barbershop, the dude gets excited. He lets Lonely know he is sure to get his hair cut there, and that he'll buzz *errbody* in the neighbourhood about it. Lonely gives him a free haircut, and gifts him an espresso. As his father likes to say, it is an auspicious beginning. It augurs well. A question: should he grow the fingernail of the little finger of his scissor hand as some Italian barbers used to do? Not exactly Edward Scissorhands, but a retro barber's classic, talented, cutting hand, it is just a thought.

Wouldn't you know it, like a ruby-throated bird, he is singing "Only the Lonely" by Roy Orbison, verse and chorus. Lonely gets off the streetcar at College and Clinton. By a hairsbreadth, he has just now sidestepped that *potentially messy situation* at Spadina Avenue on the westbound tracks, and isn't sure what mess he is stepping into with his late lunch date. Simone is already there. She wears her dirty blonde hair up in a bun on the top of her head. The bitch, as the waitress calls her when she is not calling her *putana*, has on sexy black see-through faux leather splicing crop top and body contoured shorts. She doesn't have much time for lunch and says so. Once they meet up, they kiss with snaking tongues, (Lonely knows the technique), grope each other's bodies a bit and cling to one another, as if conjoined. They sway in, hipbone to hipbone. The waitress can see them from the patio.

"Get a fucking room," she says, as if she knows what she is talking about.

They are in the Café Del Popolo, *the People's Café*, at the corner, or for lovers of short form and Bebop, *the Del Pop*, but for the hip, *the Café Dip*[2]. Lonely tells the waitress, Elena D'Amico, who still has a lethal thing for him, following their obsessive fling, that he is only *half-Italian*. When she asks him which half (top or bottom), because she thinks she already knows, he sternly rebukes her, telling her to keep *things* to herself with a hard look and particular gesture she also knows so well. As for her, she is, top half and bottom half, about 5 foot 4 with spiked heels on. Elena is playing with her hair, a short, black bob, which makes her look a little like Juliette Binoche, according to the cook that she has nicknamed the Falcon. He calls her an *upside down woman*. He has just said to her face, and she can't believe it without sticking

2   For patrons and passersby, less than kind, and even nostalgic, it was the *Café Dee Pee*.

a fork into his head, just minutes before, while she is picking up an order, that she looks like a woman who has been bound and gagged, tied upside down from the ceiling, in a straightjacket bondage getup, or should be. She is that uptight, who knows? The cook says she needs to chill, not get her panties in a knot, and relax. He says she should save it up for a dirty weekend and calls her *Elena di Troia, Helen of Troy*. With that classical reference, he is calling her a *slut*, Italian-style. So she gives him one with a flick of a finger, and another with a knee to his aproned groin. She has her reasons for saying these things, and doing what she is doing to assert herself and save face. She is simply pointing out just *who* is walking in and sitting down, as if nothing has happened between them before Lonely has started mailing it in.

"No sex is ever enough or good enough when love dies," the Falcon reminds her, doubled-over, groaning, cupping his balls, like a defender in a soccer match.

"And get a load of *who* the hell he is *with*," Elena says, all jumped-up. "What a *beating*."

Her skin is burned dark by the Adriatic sun from a recent cruise. Still flaking, she tears off a patch with sharp fingernails and puts it between her teeth, then spits it to hit the Falcon's face. Truth is: the trip has failed to relax her, even by half. The woman he is with, Simone, now making Lonely moan, as far as the waitress can tell, isn't half anything. Maybe, top half. Maybe, half Portuguese and half something else: Slavic, probably Polish, if Elena is to venture a guess, and she does. She is always good at guessing and half-guessing, with a sneer, but the cook calls it jealousy.

Simone orders a slice. Lonely gets the veal cutlet sandwich, as usual, with just a little sauce. The waitress asks Simone, trying to mess with her, if she wants anything to *drink*. Then lists what she has, as if they are poisons: mineral water, Brio, beer, wine, and coffee. Simone opts for a macchiato, coffee stained with foamed milk, or the other way around, depending on the bitterness and spite of the Barista. Elena is working the bar, too. Lonely has a double espresso short. He eats fast, as always, and finishes eating first. The waitress comes back, circles round, hovers over them with malicious intent, as the cook observes, and makes shrill and idle chitchat, on purpose, often in dark whispers, half Italian dialect, half broken English.

"Do you remember the 2014 World Cup?" she asks, as if interrogating them.

"Sure do," Lonely says, stoked. "It went sour for Portuguese fans."

"Especially here at the Café," the waitress says. "The team lost to Germany 4-0."

"What if they were playing the Italian National Team?" Lonely pipes in, trying to shoo Elena off, but the waitress won't fly, and nobody, especially a cheating pile of shit with shit covered in shit flies, like Lonely, can ever make her buzz off.

"When Italy battled England," she is telling Simone, "we charged the customers a little extra."

"Fifteen bucks per fan per hour," Lonely says, trying to despise her. "Fifteen bucks per fan per hour."

"You can't just warm the seat," the waitress says, still feeling the pangs. "You gotta *pay*."

"I always *pay*," he says, giving her his male gaze, eyes clenched like white-knuckled fists.

"Man, we had you eating and drinking at $15.00 an hour. You *got off* cheap."

As far as Lonely is concerned, she is just singing *Figaro*.

"The girl's insane," the waitress hears him say, but she makes him watch the movement of her hips, and listen to her high-heeled pumps click in a quick getaway.

Later, when she slaps the check on the table, circles it clockwise and counter-clockwise, slides it back and forth, knowing Lonely won't pick it up and pay, Simone traps it with long, lacquered fingernails in a spidery configuration and pays the bill.

"Good luck on the shop," the waitress says, "that is, if it ever opens. See you around, Lonely." She flashes Simone her lipstick-stained teeth, and whispers his name again with a long, exhaled breath: "*Lonely*."

He can live with the *moniker* and nickname as long as he can make the shop happen, no backlash in the community, no identity crisis. Any identity is better than no identity at all. Still, he is touchy about the handle if it is already a joke in Little Italy.

"*Go moan*," the waitress murmurs, as they do in the neighbourhood. Or is it *Go moan, alone* as in that book she likes to read?

When Simone makes for the exit, Lonely leans across the table to scoop up the generous tip she has left, and shoves the coins into the <u>right back pocket</u> of his tight pants for safekeeping, as if the waitress isn't watching. He thinks it is going to be an all-day date, including fringe benefits in a parking lot. To his way of thinking, Simone has left too big a tip, especially for such a sawed-off know-it-all waitress like Elena in thigh-high stockings and stiletto heels. The only tip she deserves is *to keep her mouth shut*. Besides, you never know when you are going to need small change. The waitress is only guessing or half-guessing, but it likely goes like this:

"Gelato?" Lonely asks Simone in front of the Sicilian Sidewalk Café.

"Melon flavor," she says.

"You're not going to get melon here," he says.

"Maybe some other place," she says.

"Maybe nowhere," Lonely says. "Maybe Italy. It's all just FOMO, *fear of missing out.*"

"I'm not afraid of anything," Simone says, "and I'm not missing out."

"I'm here, Simone," Lonely breaks out, stressing the vowels, "for the Spumoni."

They settle for spumoni and pistachio ice cream. Lonely pays, shelling out from the tip money. It is only right. Simone eats her scoop out of a cup. Lonely has a cone. It is hot, sweltering. The cone is dripping. The melting cone drips down the front of his black T-shirt and dribbles along the crotch of his form-fitting black jeans. They head down Grace Street, a block away from his unopened barbershop, *The Lonely Barber*. If things work out, he'll see about taking her there. The shampoo trick, the trim, the bangs, the tousled hair, and the mirror dance, they seldom if ever fail in the barber's not so subtle art of seduction.

"Where you taking *me*?" Lonely wants to know.

If Simone doesn't have a place in mind, he sure does. She keeps looking back over her naked shoulder. Lonely thinks she is taking him for sure to Trinity Bellwoods Park, south of Dundas Street. He tells her he is jealous of her already, jealous of her past, jealous of her future. He steals that line from his ex. If things get serious between them, and if things go beyond a make-out session, he wants *things* his way, and always will.

"Don't care for jealous guys," Simone says, edgy. "They try to control you."

"Control, fuck," he says. "What are they calling it now?"

"*Co-dependency?*"

"Right, but that's *what* it *is*, and *what* it is *is how* it is. Still, it's love or it isn't. You fill me and I fill you, or we're done."

Yet Lonely doesn't get to finish. Two or three guys, casting long hyper-charged shadows, jump him and knock him to the ground. His cone splats in the dirt soon covered with ants. Bees buzz in. Lonely is stung, kicked and punched. He keeps looking over at the smashed cone. Where is Simone? The shadows drag him to an alley and throw him up against a wall. Lonely is a dwarf in the Dwarf Tossing Competition at the Leopard Lounge in Windsor the way he remembers tossing a dwarf. Scissors, knives, hammers, bats, axes, stones, that's how they sound and feel like when they try to cut him, bleed him and break his bones. That's what they want the beating to feel like. Lonely can't see his assailants—what with the black sack over his head. Then the brow takes a blow, blunt force, breaks open, and bleeds. An ear bitten into, will they rip it off? They pack him into the back of a black Hummer and speed off.

Lonely doesn't know where he is. What the fuck has happened to Simone? He narrates the chain of events that has brought him here to a short, squat, powerfully built, silver-haired man, asking him questions he can't answer, because his head is suffocating in a black sack, and Lonely's mouth is full of blood and loose teeth.

"Talk," the old man says, hitting Lonely on the side of the face and making his ear buzz.

"Free me. Where's Simone?"

"The woman you were with got away," the old man says. "Lucky for her."

"Who's talking?" Lonely demands. "Her deadbeat dad? A jealous ex, or pimp, or both?"

An open hand hits him in the back of the head. Can you slap a guy to death? If Lonely can only get his hands on the straight razor, then it will be no contest.

"I just picked her up. Agreed to meet at the Café Dip, Del Pop, Dee Pee, depending on your sass."

"Keep talking till you get it right. By the way, I'm Pietro d'Arborio," the interrogator says.

"The *Shoemaker*? Lonely sputters, but he already knows him, just as everybody does in the neighbourhood, not just as a local tyrant, but also Elena's grandfather and her family's patriarch.

2. NO POLICE

Lonely splutters spitting blood. He starts telling his side of the story to stay alive. Stories are survival. He doesn't fight back. He can't, he is *trapped*. His hands are already cut up from a knife fight from last week and never mind what has just happened to him. It is like living the same day over and over again. He tells *Pietro* (or is it *Mr. d'Arborio*, or *the Shoemaker*, at this stage of the interrogation?) that his hands are a mess. He needs his hands to ply his trade. Lonely has been eating an ice cream cone, just for the cool sweetness of licking it with his long tongue on a Toronto hot summer's day. That is when they jump him, kick his head in, and, though his head doesn't get stuffed into a black sack as in today's incident, the threat feels the same as the one last week. He calls it a foreshadowing of events. By his own admission, the thing of it is that he doesn't want to let go of the cone. One guy is on top, wailing on him, and the other guy is just watching.

He is on his back, and his arms are flailing, and this goddamn bee comes buzzing around his bloody face, and his balls, and buzzing around what is left of his ice cream cone. He tells it to buzz off, but it doesn't. It won't. Does the Shoemaker happen to know why? It is the Queen Bee. Looking for sweetness, she mistakes his privates for a honeycomb. It is another case of mistaken identity. In his condition, Lonely doesn't catch the bee. The Queen is free to return to the palace of her hive and mount the throne of her Royal Jelly.

"Just like Simone," the Shoemaker says.

"A loser is a loser, right?" Lonely says.

How has Lonely been mistaken for some other unknown loser, a nonentity, who badly needs a good beating? What has he done? Steal his girl, Simone? Or insulted the waitress at the Café Del Pop? Lonely has dated Elena a couple of times, stays with her for a while, moves in, and, as quickly, when he has to, moves out, so as to move on. Their living together is a bad romance. He says she is too clingy, too intense, too fast. He hasn't exactly dumped her, but let things cool off and just fade to black. She still thinks it is too sudden, too violent. Has she told her grandfather? Is this what the beating is about? But you can't be expected to return every call and answer every text and email with so much to do in city life. Besides, is that enough to get a man tortured and killed? Something has to happen, right? Somebody has to pay when the time comes for a reckoning. The Shoemaker, the reckoner, doesn't believe the ice cream story and the bit about the cone. He tells Lonely to cut the Queen Bee routine, and drop the Lonely Barber act. At the time, he doesn't know about Lonely and his granddaughter, Elena.

"You're only *nobody*," the Shoemaker says, taking the black sack from off Lonely's head, "the loneliest of lonely barbers in Little Italy. They find your lonely feet still in your running shoes, floating in the lake, and never know whose."

The Shoemaker unties his hostage, like untying a tight knot of the gnarled shoelaces from a pair of runners dangling from telephone wires overhead. White tennis shoes, Queen St. W. and Callender St. Grey Adidas runners, Keele St. and Junction Rd. Brown leather boots, alleyway off Humbert St., just west of Ossington Ave. Blue Adidas high tops, Baldwin St. and Augusta Ave. And don't forget the running shoes dangling high above Crestfallen Lane.

Lonely knows now where he is: in the barbershop, Lonely's own place, *The Lonely Barber*. The Shoemaker shows him the key to explain how he has let himself in, no broken windows or popped locks. Besides, he knows this shop. He has worked as a shoemaker for 30 years in that site-specific cobbler shop. The skinny is that he used to deal dope by putting it in the shoes and boots he patches and mends. Invisible mending is his specialty. Good as new, you never even see the patch. They have nicknamed him the *Bootlegger*, but he prefers the *Shoemaker*. Is his dealing an urban legend, a neighborhood rumour, a shield, and a front? He has connections at City Hall, knows the laws and bylaws, and can pay his legal fees, and pay for his mistakes. He has secured the place in perpetuity. Amen.

The Shoemaker is shuffling a deck of Italian cards, as if doing card tricks. He has to play dirty, and he does. Lonely wants out of there, but he knows that the Shoemaker has posted his Hummer-driving Shadows outside.

"Look, why don't you let me give you a shave and a haircut? Let me make you an espresso. We can forget about the whole thing, the kidnapping, the beating and interrogation. No police, right?"

"Just forget about it?" asks the Shoemaker. "I suppose you want me to make you a pair of shoes, put some dope inside the hollow heels, or repair your old shoes with invisible mending, so you can just walk away?"

"Now we understand each other," says Lonely. "People walk away, no hard feelings."

Tit for tat, *quid pro quo*, one hand washes the other, the way it always is in Little Italy.

"So what's this about? You got the wrong guy."

"This can take a long time. Or be cut short, and you can go."

"Simone."

"Right. Now, what about her?"

"My guess is that you don't want me to see her."

"Keep talking."

"That she's no good. You showed me *something* about Simone."

"What?"

"That she would run out on me, and she did."

"What do you know, you're smarter than you look."

"So let me go. You proved your point."

"There's something else."

"What else? This shop? It used to be yours."

"Used to be?"

"All right, you're letting me know, in no uncertain terms, that you still *own* it, no matter what."

"It's a shoemaker's shop."

"I'm waiting to hear."

"You'll hear."

"Anything else I should know? Can I walk out of here? No police. No police."

"Who's worried about the police?"

"Unless Simone has already made a call."

"If I know her, and I think I do, and her rap sheet, which is another way of owning her ass, she won't be dialing up the police."

"No, I guess not."

"Not for a nothing like you. But, as we used to say: *What are you going to do about it—go complain City Hall?*"

3. The New Boo

Simone sees them in the shadows, Rocco (Malandrino) Spacone and Deodato (Rospo) Fiorentino, two of the shady gang working in the shadows and the alleys for Pietro d'Arborio, the Shoemaker. She sees their black Hummer parked in the lane. Though she watches them running across the street, they keep their distance at the café and ice cream shop. Once she and Lonely hit Grace Street, they simply move in like wild dogs. To get away, Simone runs down the alley behind St. Francis of Assisi Church. It is too bad about Lonely. Yet she assumes he can handle himself. His broken nose makes him look like a prizefighter. Still, there are two or three of them holding him down. She wants to stay to fight for him, but thinks better of it. She is packing, but needs more ammo. Like Elena, Simone always carries a weapon, especially on dates. You have to beat men at their own game. She knows the Shoemaker is looking for her. He is a controlling and jealous ex-lover, a jilted sugar daddy, and no longer young. She can't dump his old, sorry ass, even when she tries. Going out with other guys doesn't work either. Betrayal only makes him more determined to hold on to what he thinks he still owns. He is charming at first, like all *shoemakers*, but then becomes someone else. They always begin with charm and end with bodily harm. Simone knows that the Shoemaker will stop at nothing to get information out of you, not even the boot. Little or nothing changes with a jealous guy like that, because he thinks he's perfect. It is the same when she is seeing a man named Duncan. Elena knows him, too, more than knows him. Simone likes him and he likes her. They like to meet behind the gas station or by Exhibition Place, believing d'Arborio can't find them. She thinks he will likely hate Duncan on sight. Simone has managed to keep him a secret, for his sake and hers, but doesn't know the Shoemaker already knows him and owns him. She doesn't want Duncan to get a good beating on her account, at least not then, but wait till he finds out. There are guys like Lonely (dreamers) that likely need to be bound and beaten. There are other guys like Pietro d'Arborio that like to mete out justice. There are guys like Duncan that you have to protect, for reasons of your own. They blow hot or cold. Eventually, they all just blow and blow.

They blow hard. For now, Simone has to get away from all of them and does. She does escape until she comes out at Dundas and Grace. Elena D'Amico, the waitress, is standing there waiting for her. Not all guesswork, Elena knows the escape route Simone is more than likely to take. She is there for the intercept.

"How did you know I was here?"

"Guess," Elena says, seizing her by the wrists, and pulling her arms down.

"Let go," Simone says. "Let go of me."

"Quiet down, you won't get hurt."

"Are you working for him?"

"Maybe, maybe not," Elena whispers and secures Simone's right arm, locked in hers, like a ligature.

"What's this about?"

"Your new boyfriend, my ex."

"Lonely never mentioned it," Simone says. "Though while you were serving us at the Café Del Pop, I could tell you had made it with him."

"I've got the teeth marks and bruises on my neck and breasts to prove it," Elena says.

"All guys have two sides," Simone says, as if to a sister, but her captor won't buy it.

"I just want to compare notes," Elena says. "Let you in on a little secret. Help you. Help him, if I can. Nail the sucker, if I can't. Get rid of the Shoemaker burning your ass, and if truth be told, burning all our asses with six inches of boot leather up the brown star, at the same time. That's where *you* come in."

"Didn't you like the *do* Lonely gave you? So you want him dead?"

"When he left me, I went back, tried to blow his head off. The gun jammed."

She cuts the strap of Simone's handbag.

"What did you do that for?"

"Come on, *See-Moan*," Elena says, reaches in and pulls out the handgun. "For *this*. Now move."

At this point, she doesn't pistol-whip her, but shoves her to a waiting car in front of St. Agnes Church. The door flies open. Handcuffs flash briefly in sunlight. She clamps her wrist to Simone's. Simone is pushed and then pulled into the reconditioned, red, long-finned, fishtailing 1959 Fleetwood Caddy. She gets in beside her, slams the door shut. Simone recognizes the driver. She has dated him once or twice.

"You already know the Falcon," Elena says.

"The cook at the Café," Simone says.

"Don't you remember our little hip-hop fling?" the Falcon smirks. "Caught a glimpse of you from the kitchen. I was in love. Still am. Do you like my disguise: shades with a soaring bird's eye view?"

"You can still tell who it is," Simone says.

The Falcon shifts his broad back and adjusts the rearview mirror, then checks for a close-up. He widens his big, brown eyes and opens his mouth to show his exquisite teeth. His shoulder-length raven-black hair is swept back and slicked down. He still has on his hairnet from work, and plays with it, fingers and snaps it off.

"So your Lonely's new *boo*?"

"*Just* drive," Elena says.

"Jeals," he says. "What's his real name, anyway, this Clinton Street Romeo?"

"I don't know," Simone says, straining.

"Named for a saint or something," Elena says, "but wouldn't say, and never said."

Point of fact, she knows his real name, but keeps it to herself.

"Saint Lonely," the Falcon says, "patron saint of Lonely Nobodies."

"He *ain't* no saint, as the saying goes," Elena says. "But thinks everybody is better for knowing him."

"Maybe, maybe not," the Falcon says. "Maybe, it's Martin, Marty, you know, after St. Martin de Porres, patron saint of barbers, or just Figaro. The rest is Howdy Doody. But where are Uncle Bob, Flub-A-Dub and Claribel now, if not dead, buried and gone to hell? And where's your hand puppet and *clown*, the barber? I'm just saying, and what's he really all about?"

When he finishes, he begins a line of reasoning that leads him to Lonely and what has motivated him to be a barber, anyway, and starts in on Elena.

"You're making wild *allegations*," she says, "swinging for the fences. You're offside."

"I'm just trying to figure what drives him," the Falcon says. "What's his motivation? What makes him hard? I want to get to know him better."

"You're creeping me out, man," Elena says, freaking out.

"So tell me?"

"What?"

"What's the kick with cutting hair, anyway?"

"How should I know? He's the barber."

"*Would-be,* wannabe, might be, if only, *but.* Did you ever *ask* him?"

"*Did* once. Wouldn't say. Wouldn't talk about it."

"*For* him to know and you to find out, that's him all over. He's a quiet, private, secretive type, and therefore, dangerous. Maybe, he's a hair maniac, you know, obsessed with hair, touching it, combing it, cutting and grooming it. Maybe, he eats it. Maybe, he'll give you a Mohawk, for political reasons, maybe an Up-Do. Maybe, it's personal, something to do with family history. Or it's just easy money, no responsibilities, and no homework, if you get me. He's shirking real work, all right standing on his feet all day, and cutting fifteen to twenty heads. He gets paid under the table, and then there are the tips, and skimming off the top, until the Tax Man makes a grab for his cash and coins. Am I right? But what's the thing with hair? It's intimate, maybe. He likes sweeping it up. There will be hairballs in his lungs after a lifetime of barbering. Not to mention, lice and fleas. Maybe, cooties."

"You're *weirding* me out," Elena says. "He doesn't do pubic hair, you freak."

"At this point, we don't know, *but,*" the Falcon says. "He'd be some barber, if he is trimming *quiffs.* So, maybe, he likes to satisfy his clients: satisfaction for a job well done. A good haircut makes him happy. Every head is a challenge. How many heads does he have to know, and all that? It's the story of scissors and hair. Man, he likes working with his hands. How the fuck should I know?"

"More wild allegations."

"We'll never know for sure."

"And why do you care?"

"For your sake, El, I care because you do."

"No, I don't."

"You got it bad," the Falcon says. "I care about you."

"Stick to the plan and shut your mouth," Elena says.

"You're still hard for him," he says, doing beat box, and going wild.

"What are you, a *walking* stereotype?" Simone blows up.

"First off, I'm not *walking,* I'm driving," the Falcon says. "But true, I'm longing to blow it up and leave the *past* behind me. Explode all myths and stereotypes, especially about cooks. Wait'll you get to know me better. You won't say *no* to me again. Yolo: *you only live once,* am I right, am I fucking right?"

"You give Italians a bad name," Simone says.

"He gives Italians a bad smell," Elena says, as if commenting on an old joke, a dead truth.

"It's the blood-red sauce," he says, "the Falcon's special *pomodoro* gravy. I just finished a shift in hell's kitchen at the Café."

"Shut up and drive," Elena says. "Drive."

"*Chi va piano, va sano e lontano,*"[4] says the Falcon with a sneer, but puts the pedal to the metal.

The red, Fleetwood Cadillac, its wheels burrowing their way to hell with burning rubber and clouds of smoke, hopping on its suspension, rises like a city-born peregrine falcon, and, spreading its wide wings, flies off southbound on Grace Street.

Elena is talking about the Lonely Barber. She tells them she first met Lonely at Marvel Beauty School in Yorkville, 40 hours per week of getting behind your dummy. One day, the instructor, Ms. Natasha, (Elena calls her *Don't-Touch-Me-I'm-Too-Beautiful*) takes the class down to *skid row,* Queen and Parliament. The assignment: shampoo heads and cut hair for homeless people. Elena is squeamish. She has glamour on her mind, not mercy or charity, and certainly not the possibility of lice. Lonely takes to it. He washes their hair, trims their beards and gives them hipster haircuts. She looks at him being kind to the homeless and falls for him. Maybe, he is St. Lonely. She doesn't finish beauty school. Lonely, too, takes another path, until they meet up again at the Café where she is waiting tables. She is a waitress, and he is a barber. It simplifies things, but simple is not easy.

"As from what he told me," she says, "Lonely had seen the empty shop, peach and white lilac, picture-perfect at the corner of Clinton and Mansfield. He did a quick calculation with a mental drawing and created a one-chair barbershop. He worked alone. Maybe, he would let his new girl, Elena D'Amico, work for him."

"That's *you*," says the Falcon.

"That's *me*. I was supposed to be his shampoo girl, maybe take appointments, run the shop, and later sleep with the barber. The rent was too good to be true: $450 per month."

"In the Six[5]?" screeches the Falcon. "You can't beat that for rent.

---

4   Go slowly, wisely and far.

5   The rapper, Drake, named the city *the Six.*

Was there a body buried there? Had somebody been murdered in that shop?"

"I asked him the same things," Elena says. "'I don't give a shit,' Lonely said. 'At that price, *let the dead deal with the dead.* Flip the past the bird.' There could be body parts in the pipes, my Lonely didn't care."

4. The Menu

"*Flip the past the bird*, I like that," says the Falcon, at the wheel of the 1959 Fleetwood Cadillac, fussing with his shiny-sleek, raven-black hair. "You can't argue with the *gratefully* dead. My pop's been dead, buried and rotting since forever, but I must admit, I'm still wrestling with him in my head. He wins every round. No arguing with a corpse. It's the same with couples."

"What?"

"The wrestling, I mean. When this same-sex thing came in," the Falcon is saying.

"Came in? It's always been in," says Simone."

"Why are we talking same-sex?" asks Elena.

"When it blew up, you know," he continues, "became a *thing* for coming out, I had a friend, Luciano Billycock, that came out. I wished he had stayed in, but Luciano, my friend, I asked him: 'Who was the first, you know?'"

"You thought it might be you."

"You never know, and you never know when you know at what point you really know. 'Who was your first crush?' I asked him. He said: 'Your dad.' Well, at first, I was going to smack him, you know, the way some guys say, *Your mother,* and you got to set them straight with a swift kick to the nuts, because he wasn't taking me seriously, but said: 'It was your father.' I thought it over and thought why not? He was a good-looking guy. Maybe, it could explain why he didn't get along with my mother. He would have gone crazy, if he knew *but*. A crush is a crush, am I right? Am I freaking right?"

"Freaking right," Elena says.

"That's the way it is," Simone says. "No point going ballistic: everybody loses at love."

"Earlier this morning, this couple was soaking up the sunshine on the patio," says the Falcon. "Two girlfriends, if you get my drift, and I got nothing against girl-on-girl action: lesbians, you might say. Getting friendly, cozy, you know, holding hands, playing cat's cradle, the kissing in public, but what the hell, it's a free city, and we've got safe sex and same-sex marriages at Casa Loma, right? Now, the Shoemaker doesn't go in for that sort of *thing*, doesn't like watching, not here, and especially not when he's eating a calzone. He goes up to them and lays it on them: *Not here, not in front of kids, with nonnas on the patio, and not in front of me.* So, they get confused. Nobody is doing that anymore, stopping the action, you know. A couple is a couple, right? One of them challenges the sharp-tongued critic. Everybody is drinking and smoking. Never mind the kids. He sends them to the park down the street, if they're up for a little fisting, you know."

"One of them wanted to know who was talking, who the fuck was asking," Elena says.

"The Shoemaker said he was the owner, *but,*" the Falcon says. "That's the way the old man is. He thinks he owns everything and everybody. They got up to confront him. Tell him to flip off and die, or something like that, but he looked left and right. Shadows moved. The couple took off, but not before saying the magic words: Hocus pocus, *Flip off and die.*"

"So, I started thinking," Elena says. "Flip off and die. That would look good on him."

"You're the past, Shoemaker," the Falcon says. "Flip the past the bird. Poof, you're history. You're long gone."

"When Lonely wanted the shop, the landlord told him that the place was rented by a *shoemaker*, same one, for at least 30 years."

"Pietro d'Arborio," the Falcon says, breaking up the syllables, and stressing the rhyme.

"The only tenant had been that control freak, the Shoemaker, and don't we all know it in the *neighborhood?*"

"Why did he leave?"

"Retired, I think. Maybe, *had* to leave. But he wasn't gone, not by a long shot."

"I already know all this shit about Lonely and *the Lonely Barber,*" Simone says.

"There's more," Elena says.

"Are we going to drive all day? I don't know what's up your Kardashian butt, but get to the point. What do you want? Money? I'll get it. Revenge? There's nothing serious between Lonely and me yet. The Shoemaker is making sure of that right now, if I can venture a guess, and I can, and you're likely working for him, anyway. Just what the hell do you want from me?"

"I don't know what Falconeri, the Falcon, wants," Elena says, "maybe this, maybe that, a piece is a piece, yeah, right, but he can always make a grab later. But I know what I want. I want you to *shid*[6] on the Lonely Barber."

"I always make nice," the Falcon says. "No *shidding on*. No abuse. With so much pain in the world, why add to it? What doesn't kill you makes you stronger, or kills the guy next to you, or, like the thrill on Blueberry Hill, what makes the wild heart grow fonder and fonder can make it better or deader. Besides, I can cook your favourite dishes." He starts listing a menu in hip-hop beats, rhythms and rhymes. "I can make all your favourites. For breakfast (*colazione*, if you will), I can cook you up eggs, as many as you want, bacon or sausage, toast and potato puffs with coffee or tea, French toast, bacon or sausage and potato puffs with coffee or tea, omelette, mozzarella cheese, green peppers, mushrooms, toast and potato puffs with coffee or tea, the Falcon Scrambled, two eggs, hot peppers, onions and tomato sauce. Served with toast, bacon or sausage and potato puffs with coffee or tea, the Heart-Attack, open face French toast topped with two eggs over easy served with sausage or bacon with coffee or tea, breakfast sandwich, Bacon and Egg served with potato puffs and sliced tomatoes with coffee or tea. And you can do something for me: I want you to take out Pietro d'Arborio, that cocksure cobbler, turned local tyrant."

"Take out? Kill?"

"Maim him, bleed him, castrate him, and then kill him, is fine by me. His extinction is on the menu. He's yesterday. Let the dead bury the dead. At least, give him a good emotional shit kicking. But you can't do it on an empty stomach," the Falcon says, ever the cook. "So, hear me talking now." He recommends Canadian fare, including Chicken Fingers and Fries. "Even though chickens don't have digits, etc., or Fish & Chips with fresh salad."

Again he raps a long, nauseating list of meals he can prepare. Does he do it to tantalize or to torment her?

"And all of that comes with potato puffs."

"You're reading me the goddamn menu," Simone says.

"Don't forget the Panini Sandwiches," Elena says.

"Shit, I know them by heart: with salami, capocollo, provolone, lettuce and tomato, Tuna Melt."

"On dark rye with spinach and melted Havarti."

6   Humiliate, abuse, own.

"Meatball Surprise."

"The surprise is $7.60."

"You may ask what's in it? I'll tell you."

"I'll tell her."

"All right, you say. You're the waitress."

"Hot peppers, onions and tomato sauce."

The Falcon goes on and on from there: "The latter comprises a cutlet topped with mozzarella cheese, sautéed hot pepper and onions smothered in fresh plum *pomodoro* sauce."

"I'm going to be sick," Simone says. "I get carsick. What with you're stopping and starting and non-stop talking about food. Let me out. I'm going to puke. Why are you on about the Menu? What the fuck do you want from me?"

"I already told you: I want you to *off* the Lonely Barber," Elena says. "A paper cut to his heart."

She has her reasons for saying this.

"This is our neighbourhood," the Falcon says. "It's personal. Therefore, it's political. No more bosses. No more dream-killers."

That's when she notices the camera light on the Falcon's cellphone.

"You're filming this. You're sick."

"No, you're carsick. I'm just taping the proceedings. You'll be famous. It'll go viral."

"That is, when you go postal," Elena adds.

"The whole city's a movie set," the Falcon says. "As a buff, and occasionally as part of a film crew, I can tell you that Bathurst Street (say) is like *the cerebral cortex* of a Hollywood movie. Did you ever see *Scott Pilgrim Versus the World?* The producer in his jeans, ball cap and chin stubble said so. *Hollywoodland* was shot here, but set in Los Angeles, and *Talk to Me,* shot in Toronto, was set in Washington. But I think our city can stand on its own beauty. A movie shot here and set here, Toronto is great for locations. You don't need anywhere else. Adam Egoyan knows it. He adores San Fran, for instance, and dreams of shooting there, but he can do wonders shooting *here.* Did you ever see *Chloe?* Iconic films have been shot in T.O. You can romance *the Six.* You see the Hollywood types here all the time: Julianne Moore, Liam Neeson. Toronto is ideal for movies. Think of the Rosedale ravine. Think of the Café Del Pop on College and the Rivoli on Queen. Beneath the pavements of our streets are sounds, beats, and bones. Our underground can be good to you or mean. But streetcars are veins on the skin of a beautiful body. Beauty shots: think of McCaul Street at sunset, the CN Tower, the ROM Crystal, the Luminous Veil in the twilight. Light it properly, find its sweet spots, and the city itself is a movie."

"So you're a movie buff," Simone baits him, head between her knees. "You like *watching.*"

"I like watching you."

"If this is shown to anybody, *I'll kill you.*"

"That's what I want to hear," he says. "That's the close-up I'm after and you saying, 'I'll kill you.'"

"I'm not going to *kill anybody,*" Simone says, humped over and heaving.

"You will," Elena whispers. "When we fill you in on the nature of the revenge plot, and your part in it, you'll be convinced, and you'll do what we say."

"You'll grow to like us," the Falcon predicts. "But first, kill or be killed, with kindness or no mercy. First, you need something good to eat, blood rare to get you in the mood."

"Only hurting Lonely is on this menu," Elena says.

"You're hard, El," the Falcon says.

"I was always a girl with a moustache," she says.

"So get a pluck or a shave."

"You're not man enough to pluck me or shave me. So keep your mouth shut and eyes on the road."

The Falcon drives down the maze of laneways.

"Are you trying to scare me?" asks Simone. "Is this where you're going to dump my body?"

"As good a place as any," Elena says.

"If money is what you want," Simone says.

"Keep your goddamn money," Elena says. "We're not thieves, or extortionists."

"You're kidnappers, killers," Simone says, "terrorists."

"That be different," the Falcon says. "That'd be where it's at, and what it is. And what it is *is* how it is. It's that way all over. It's fucking cruel. The city can be a cruel place. *But.*"

Though he stops, he promises to get back to the litany of cruelty later on. Elena sits close, handcuffed, to her captive. The Falcon flicks his sunglasses and drives faster and faster.

"Look, let me go," pleads Simone. "I'm really getting carsick. I'll puke."

"So puke. Nothing we haven't seen before."

Before Simone can push back, the Falcon pretends to choke a mic, as if he is in a Hip-Hop competition, more of a rap battle. He is a poet, but others don't know it, a spoken word poet. He finds a beat and adds hooks and verses. He takes advantage of rhymes for a word like "now" and rattles off "pow, pow, pow."

"So the Shoemaker is a smalltime dealer," Simone says, breathing hard, "like the rest of us. Only he's got connections with City Hall, and we don't. He owns Little Italy. You want me to zap him?"

"Make him moan, Simone."

The Falcon makes to choke and swallow his pretend mic. Then goes on with the beats, the rhythms of rap and rhyming with mic drop quotes.

"The King must die. Long live the Queen."

"You know who the King is," Elena says.

"Who's the *Queen*?" Simone screams, and pukes.

"You are," Elena bawls out.

"Long live Queen Simone," the Falcon, fist-pumping the air, gives her a hip-hop shout out.

"Get me out of here," Simone vomits into her mouth.

"Here's my *thing*: *it's the* speed-of-violence," the Falcon is saying about the city. "How does it get there so fast? V-i-o-l-e-n-c-e, violence, the shootings on Boxing Day, the gun play at the Eaton's Centre, the knifings in schools and alleyways, clubs and parties, home invasions, assaults and gang wars? What are we going to say? 'We are Toronto.' Tinted glasses reflect fierce negotiations. A shot-up poker game gambles on deception and doubles the wild card. Reflectors take in bloodstained sunsets. A dealer with mirrored glasses cuts marked cards, and plays for the sake of the trick, and his double-cross takes in any cheater's refracted light, like a motor-cycle cop with mirrored glasses for your arrest. *Happiness was a warm gun* until the *Summer of the Gun.* But how does it get there so fast? At 33,000 feet, duct-taped to her seat, it gets worse than this in less than a breath, for the girl under arrest. It hurts just looking at her. She wears a double-hooded spit mask. They say she's breaking bad. No negotiations, only speed and its need to control, to hurt. Where's the stun gun? Instead of stunning her, they say: '*Stop resisting, or I'll duct-tape your face.'* They kill a kid on the streetcar— plug him nine times. Then gunfire on the Hill ricochets off our vigilant

City Hall and subway walls. To the sounds of self-radicalized men, security is beefed up with S.W.A.T. teams and lockdown. But how does violence get there so fast?"

"I'm not listening," Elena says. "I'll show you violence if you don't stop."

"I stopped listening at 'It's *the speed,*'" Simone says.

"You agree I'm making a point here, right?" asks the Falcon.

"What point?"

"Views of the city," he says. "Have you ever taken a good, hard look? Two Views of the same city: crazy town (Ford Nation), or like Naples, *see it and die,* or *see the Six and live.* What holds everything back, slow misunderstandings, crawling along tagged walls, walking our bikes with flat tires, if they don't get stolen, even as the story holds us away from the same moment together, always twice, two views of the same thing, dispute of time and place, disgrace of killing the story, not living it, before we put our names to it. Then spin of the white nights (not *satin* as in the song by the Moody Blues), but the curated White Night in the curated city on *Nuit Blanche,* liquid crystal projects on alley walls, the street performances rivaling the daylight madness of artists preaching art, in two views of the city at night, getting rid of darkness, staying up all night long so the homeless can finally get some merciful sleep, dreaming up the place, two views of the same city."

"Let's get on with it," Elena insists. "She's going to have to clean up her mess."

"About the puke," the Falcon says, "I recommend Schweppes: more fizz, better burps."

"No ginger ale," says Elena. "It's not on the menu: no fizz and no burps for the likes of her."

5. SHADOW DOGS

Two-thirty in the afternoon. The reconditioned 1959 Fleetwood Cadillac is heading south, as if to the Leslie Street Spit, who knows, maybe the Toronto Harbour, as if en route to making a drop or dumping a body. They keep messing with Simone, holding her on a short, tight leash and jerking it from time to time, but, despite the threat, hostility and menace, still speaking from their lacerated hearts.

"But here's the thing about my *thing*," the Falcon says, from the deepest point of his heart's core. "What would be lost if we lost the city? What wouldn't I give to do a rap of what was lost then found, a drift of hogs, trotters trotting back to haunt Muddy York? I'd give you trees standing in the water. Post a letter to a lone mailbox on Yonge Street, longest road in the country. Through *the narrows,* I'd dedicate poles and nets to the route connecting Lake Ontario to Simcoe. In the spring run of walleye, pike, sucker, and sturgeon, I'd fish for my origins. To chart the worth of city life, even its wilderness and dark places, its hauntings and subterranean ways. To record it in flashes of 360 degrees from the Edgewalk of the CN Tower, gallery of exploding suns. To read it as a fictional city, all-seeing views in the hyper-charge of the city, rooted here, rarer than the way the Path runs underground, or earthed at the mouth of the Humber River, recalling how once cars and bathers washed in the same stream. Or else I'd get the fuck out of here."

"Shut up about that shit," Elena says. "You're wasting time. We've got to be careful. They're likely to sic the shadow dogs on us."

"Woof, woof. What are you saying: an attempt on our lives?"

"It's only logical. I mean it's what I'd do."

"Not the first attempt on my life, and I'm sure it won't be the last."

"They ordered a hit on you? What for?"

"Let's say not everybody likes what you cook and serve up for them in the Café or in life. Last summer, I spent a couple of days at the house of one of our old group in the High Park area. I knew I shouldn't have gone out to the west end. Best to stay where you're staying. Anyway, my pal, Sal, had thought it was a good idea, because he had been getting death threats for some card game he had won or lost or some local political shit that he had run foul of, I don't know, and needed somewhere to hole-up and hide. He accepted an invitation to housesit for a shady *friend* who was supposed to be vacationing in Italy, and asked me to come along. Sal didn't really know the guy. But he saw it as a quick adventure, and a way of taking a break from running, and for me, a chance to play billiards in a rich guy's house, drink his booze, barbecue meat and swim in the pool. 'Use the place as long as you like,' was on the card. It was signed: "P." When we got there, we saw other *houseguests* strolling on the lawn, or swimming in the jumbo pool. Sal's absent friend made a point of leaving his house to special *acquaintances*. I'd never seen such wealth, and also such generosity and trust. I mean would you let just anybody use your house?"

"I would," Simone says.

"Well, okay, so you're that kind, but you don't know Sal, and you don't really know me. So, a son-of-a-bitch named Angelo Disgraziato, or something like that (Sal treated him with respect), came into the room and joined us. It made me panicky, jumpy. I felt uncomfortable. Angelo and Sal sat in plush chairs, in shirtsleeves, legs crossed like rich bastards, drinking cognac. A stiff guy, dressed in a tux, had brought in glasses. You know, snifters. The windows looked like church windows: you know, stained glass. 'You should be shot in the head,' Angelo said. 'It wouldn't be the first time, and it certainly won't be the last,' Sal said. 'I've survived several attempts just this month.' He wasn't exaggerating. There had been death threats and several close calls. 'I'm a marked man,' he said. 'I'm like a held note.' We laughed and continued to drink cognac and just talk. The three of us then went out for a walk on the grounds of the estate. Everything was shrubberies, fountains and statues. 'This is fantastic.' This and that, we walked through the rose garden, and then through the *arboretum* (yeah, fuck, I'll never forget it) with its luminous woody plants and its drift of conifers. 'Our absent host is nuts,' Angelo said. 'Would you invite guests to your home, give them everything they want, and then leave for Italy? His invitation couldn't have come at a better time for me personally.' By the outdoor pool, he confessed that he didn't really know his host. He'd met him at a party and had spent an evening or two drinking with him in Toronto. 'Despite his money,' he said, 'he has sympathy for the poor and for political activists. Our evenings consisted of talking about how much money he had given to free political prisoners around the world and how much capital he had invested in supplying weapons for revolutionary causes. One night, he had brought with him several whores that he insisted were militants working for somebody. I said to myself: If our friend is a voyeur with a taste for danger, then I'll *perform* for him with skill.' 'And are you a whore?' asked Sal. 'You'll have to find out for yourself,' said Angelo. 'But that night, I was.' Once in the pool, I stared at a girl whose long hair flowed down her back. In a clearing, the musicians, mostly women, played blindfolded. Dinner was being served. I heard a bell tolling. We entered the house through a wing that had the appearance of a hall of mirrors, like at the Ex in the old days. We were escorted to a dining hall where close to forty people were seated around a huge, freaking table. I liked what I saw. Sal didn't. 'A feast,' I said. I wanted to cook that spread. We began eating right away. I watched everyone as they joked and laughed and ate. Maybe, this is paradise, I thought. Everything you want with the host, absent. We were served many things, all of which were well prepared. The *hors d'oeuvres* that the guests consumed consisted of such things as: *champignons farcis, trempette au fromage et au piment, Quiche Lorraine, boulettes aux crabes, paté de foie gras.* Drinks were served chilled, or at room temperature, as desired, especially for the wine. 'Can you name what everyone is drinking?' asked Angelo. Another game. 'That drink, for instance. 'An Alexander,' replied Sal. 'Good, and that?' 'A Bloody Mary.' 'Now this one?' 'A Daiquiri, and that is a *Sauterelle,* and that is a Scarlet O'Hara.' 'Very good,' said Angelo. I was drinking a beer. The meal consisted of steaming meats and luxurious breads, *étouffé aux crevette,* a kid prepared in milk, a zucchini omelette, cheese custard, a rice fluff, stuffed squid, spinach salad, cucumber mousse, roast pork, lambs' brains, pigeon, roast duck, eels, and quails."

"They were eating birds?" asks Simone, puking up more mucus.

"Quails, everyone could choose the amount and the variety of food desired," the Falcon says, "even birds. Wines were served, white, red, sparkling and dry. For dessert: *Sorbet à la crème et à l'orange, Toubien aux cerise, Gelatin frappé,* Chocolate *soufflé,* Strawberry *torte, Flan à l'ananas, Beauté noir, Pots de crème.* The liqueurs included *Café de Paris, Crème de Menthe,* Brandy, Cognac, and so on. When we got up from the table, we felt excited and exhausted. Sal felt sick. He let the sound of his pleasure burst in the air behind him. A beautiful woman informed us that private entertainment awaited us in our private rooms. 'Who has been inside my brain?' I asked. 'Who knows my fantasy life and is feeding my afflictions?' The woman smiled. We went upstairs, and several women greeted us. They were lookalikes and dressed like screen legends from the past, I don't know, goddesses. In these disguises, they sat and talked with us. I spoke timidly to Laura Antonelli. Sal caressed Sophia Loren. Angelo talked to Monica Vitti. He still could not decide which one he wanted. The women poured us some wine. Sal played something for them on the piano, a jazz improvisation. Later, totally drunk, they danced. I was now with Sophia Loren, and Sal had been seducing Monica Vitti, and was in turn seduced by her. Angelo lay on the floor with the rest of them. Exhausted, I struggled to get up. I wanted to go to bed. One of the celebs got up to go with me. But I stopped her. Before I got to the door, Sal put his arm around my shoulder and said: 'It is a good thing that you gave up on her. Poor Angelo, tomorrow he'll wake up in the arms of an impostor, a fake. Yes, he's probably used to being tied up, and I'm sure he's aware of his own latency and repression, but he'll burn in a fire that will completely consume him, if he chooses her.' They were all fakes. I vomited in the hall. (Sorry, Simone.) Found my way to the bedroom and collapsed on the bed. The next morning, I discovered Laura Antonelli and Monica Vitti sleeping next to me. I got up and went into the bathroom. Vomited and washed. I left the room quietly. There was no need to dress. I had fallen asleep in my clothes. Sal got up after only a few hours of sleep and said: 'Get me out of here. I'm burning up. I'm going to puke out what's left of my brains.' Since I didn't have my wheels, I called a cab, and we waited for it outside on the front steps. When it arrived, we got in and told the cabbie to head to College Street. A shot rang out. It had been a set-up. Just then, a bullet from a high-powered weapon ricocheted off the marble steps and landed in the driveway. Angelo was in the bushes trying to reload. He had drunk too much and had missed his intended target, my pal, Sal. The host wouldn't be pleased. Sal's hired killer had failed again to kill him."

"Why are you telling us this shit?" Elena says. "It never even happened."

"It did," the Falcon insists. "If Sal was still on this side of the grass (he got plugged a week later), I'd get him to tell you himself."

"You're full of surprises," Simone says.

"And full of shit," Elena says.

"All right, I admit I embellished a bit, as they say, but why can't a cook be a storyteller with tales from the kitchen?" the Falcon says. "Why not admit it makes a fucking good story to tell while we're waiting to get the job done, especially when we're waiting around, getting in the mood for an assassination? You know, I always had a bad feeling that the Shoemaker was behind the attempt."

"You're freaking out," Elena says. "I knew I shouldn't have brought you in on this."

"I'm just saying," the Falcon says. "Can't a dude have a thought, and have his say?"

"You're losing it," Elena says. "Keep it together."

"Still not listening?" he asks Simone.

"You're trying to have a thought," she says. "Only you can't think straight. Don't strain yourself too much, but you're welcome to keep trying. You puke your puke. I puke mine."

"Thanks," he says. "I knew you were listening. And I *know*."

"What?"

"That even though you're giving me the stink eye," the Falcon says, "you're starting to like me."

"In your dreams," Simone says.

"In my dreams," he says, "I'm dreaming about you. It's my waking dream. One day, you'll dream about me, too. By the way, that's the most puke I've ever seen. As I said, you're gonna need some ginger ale. Or else I'll be like that Octopus I heard about the other day that got away on eight legs from its enclosure and slithered to a sewer nearby and made good its escape to the ocean, its home, and got its slimy ass and eight hairy legs out of there."

"Shut up," Elena says. "They're likely to sic the shadow dogs on us. And you, Simone, stop moaning and clean up your mess."

Shots ring out, ricochet off the speeding, red caddy making its ballistic get-away.

The Falcon drives on, and then Elena talks about the way to hurt Lonely.

"You confiscated my gun," Simone says, moaning.

"I disarmed her," Elena tells the Falcon.

"Women can be so violent," he says.

"No gun. What am I supposed to use?"

"*This*," Elena says and holds up an envelope.

"You want me to kill him with paper cuts?"

"The *letter*," Elena says. "*The* Letter from City Hall."

"The bad news will *kill* him, so to say," says the Falcon. "Shut him down, so to say, at least, that's the theory. No guns, just a thrill-kill with un*kindness*."

"What *kind* of revenge is that?" demands Simone. "No revenge at all."

"The coldest possible," Elena says, "served on a cold plate."

"By a waitress you once slept with, then dumped," says the Falcon.

"News comes and you read it," Elena says. "Then you fold the letter and ache to cut your throat with it. Somebody has refused you. Somebody you don't know has killed your dream. That's the kind of revenge I'm after."

Elena twists her arm and turns Simone towards the window.

"Look at it," Elena insists.

"At what?"

"Look at the city," the Falcon suggests. "Look at the Tower. Am I right? Of course, I'm fucking right. It's beautiful. Some say our city is a cruel place. But cruelty is not the city's fault. Whose fault is it? In this story, it's a shoemaker's. They're changing his city, and he feels he has the right to take it back."

Driving, the Falcon films the city with his cellphone.

"You're both cruel," Simone says.

"Cruel?" Elena shouts. "You're such a *beating*: you think you're better than everybody else. You cheat on and mistreat guys, and you say we're *cruel*. With all the stories and rumours buzzing around, regarding how you treat those drones, you think you're the Queen Bee."

"What rumours? What stories?"

"Let me get this straight," Elena says. "Men come at you, and boys in an earlier time, as if they want you (or expect you) to kick them in the balls."

Simone doesn't say anything. She knows it is a kind of provocation. Whatever she says will likely set Elena off. She won't take the bait. It is best not to speak or try to defend herself.

"So Simone would oblige them," the Falcon says. "She would kick them between the legs, not for the fun of it, but as a kind of gift, a way of meeting expectations, obligingly, as it were, *that's for you because you want me to,* you know, that sort of thing, *and are asking for it.*"

"Men are always asking for it."

"Were they always asking for it? Or were you dishing it out because you have contempt for men?"

"They expect to cry," the Falcon says, "and she makes them cry, from the pit of their guts, the way I cry over love and loss, from deep in the groin, they weep for her, I can understand that."

"At her cruelty," Elena says, "at her betrayal, at her contempt for them."

"So they convince themselves," the Falcon says. "She likely had to say she hated their guts or they weren't ever satisfied, don't you see? Men crawl on all fours for it"

"Lonely was no different, I suppose," Elena says.

"She was the sweetness they wanted, Lonely included, I'm sure," he says. "They always hinted at it. You know, sweet angel this and honey that. She was their angel. I can see that happening. But she was never *Simone* to them, just Simone. That's what she wanted, am I right? That's what *you* wanted, didn't you, Simone?"

"Keep talking," Simone says. "You love to hear yourselves mouthing off. But the more you say, the more you miss it."

"What are we missing exactly?" asks Elena. "What's up with you, and how you got yourself in this predicament?"

"You miss it, you miss it," Simone says. "And about me, you miss out."

"I'm not missing out," Elena says. "And the Falcon never misses anything. He's got those eyes of his that can see things miles and miles away; a bird of prey."

"You're not talking about me," Simone says, "but yourselves. This whole thing is about you, not me. Yet you're convinced you got it down and that you figured me out and know my past and shit. Nothing to know, you're just making it up as you go along, like the rest of us do."

"Let's go back," Elena says, not wanting to hear her out. "It's getting late for revenge."

"Clinton Street," the Falcon laughs, "home of *The Lonely Barber.*"

The Falcon revs the engine, and, screeching and screaming, the Fleetwood Cadillac flies north to *The Lonely Barber.* Elena guesses or half-guesses where Lonely is: her grandfather has him in for a good beating in the shop. It serves them both right. Armed with the revenge *letter*, they intend nothing else but to dump on Lonely with a *Special Delivery* drop.

6. Scene of the Crying

In the clash, growing darker and going blue, holed up in the unopened barbershop for the past three or three and a half hours, a line of reasoning starts that leads to the matter of *life in the city*.

"City Life," Lonely says, "city life, that's the only word for it. City life seems kind of sweet sometimes. Yes, a bit bitter from time to time, I'll grant you that. Yes, but I think the key is not letting the blanket of bitterness cover you up too soon. If you do, you'll walk around like something out of Edgar Allan Poe, walking around in your shroud, believing you're alive, but you're just a dead man walking. The point is: not to sink completely into your grave when hard times come, God-awful times, when no hope is to be seen, heard, smelt, felt, dealt. I'm not saying it won't come. It'll come, Mr. d'Arborio, it'll come. Give it time. Life, life can be much sweeter I think. It can be better than this. They want to fuck with you and screw you over. Do their best to squeeze every last breath right out of you. But you got to hold on. That's right, hold on, even when they beat you down and grab you by the throat and press a boot down on your face and piss on you. My advice is keep your head down and don't react. Weather the storm, Mr. d'Arborio, like any good shoemaker, or any artisan. Let the sun come up. Let the sun in. I love the way the sun lifts with the morning on College Street, the way it comes into the alley when you pick yourself up and clean off the snot and dried blood from your swollen face. Nothing sweeter, nothing sweeter than spitting out a tooth or two and getting on with the day."[7]

"Right, right, the sweetness of life, but I'll let you in on a little secret," the Shoemaker says, blowing a tiny whistle dangling around his neck from a gold chain to make his point, or maybe signaling his Shadows stationed outside the shop, or both. "I know what you're up to, and it won't work."

What does a shoemaker know? Then again, shoemakers have always haunted Lonely's life story. Once his grandfather on his dad's

Based on dialogue from *Jokers Wild* by Nic
Labriola

side becomes a shoemaker, he meets Lonely's grandmother. Turns out, her papa is a shoemaker, too. They marry. The shop prospers, until he abandons it, sells or gives away his tools, the apron, the leather, the last, the hammers, the nails, and comes to Canada. That's on his father's side. Now, on his mother's side, his grandfather stretches the truth a little and says he's a shoemaker just to get a job with Bata Shoes after the war. So, they want to see what he can do. He butchers the leather and fashions a shoe that looks like a catcher's mitt. He's fired on the spot. Years later, Lonely's grandfather makes a wallet from an old boot. But there's no need for his craft and handiwork at the time. Still, shoemakers have haunted Lonely's whole life.

"What am I'm up to?" Lonely asks. "Just trying to set up a shop."

"*You* need a license," the Shoemaker says.

"I applied," Lonely spits out. "I know I need a fucking license."

"Say you want in on anything in this city from adult entertainment to old gold dealer, *you need a license.*"

"I applied," Lonely says, exhaling, "for a goddamn barbershop license."

The Shoemaker tells Lonely that he is stumbling around this good city getting into mischief, because he's weak and stupid. No head for business, his head is not even up his ass, because he doesn't know which end is up. Or it's so far up his ass that if he pinches his cheeks together, he'll cut off his head. Or he can't find his ass with both hands and all the lights on. The Shoemaker gets up into Lonely's face and says that every card has two faces and so do people: every scene, every situation, two faces, straight up or upside down. So there they are, face-to-face, two men going head-to-head in a one-chair, unlicensed barbershop, telling over and over a story that they can't finish.

"I'm calling you out," the Shoemaker says.

"What do you want? Protection money?"

"If I wanted your money, I wouldn't need to get involved."

"Are you just flexing your muscles? Declaring who is boss?"

"I'm boss, plenty of muscle, no flexing necessary."

"You're playing with me to mess with Simone, right?"

"Maybe, maybe not."

"Show her she can't get away from you."

"There's nowhere to go."

"Let me go, and I won't even go back to the scene of the crying."

"Scene of the *crying?*"

"Scene of the crime. CRIME."

"You said, *Crying. Mortacci tui.*[8]"

"I said, *Scene of the crime.* What's the matter with you?"

"Nothing you can understand."

"Look, I promise I won't go back to the scene of the *crime*," Lonely says.

"Where the crying took place," insists the Shoemaker.

"No, back to the *place* where they jumped me."

"You didn't cry? You didn't beg for mercy on your knees and ball your yellow eyes out? Vomit ice cream all over a flock of seagulls?"

Lonely keeps his mouth shut. He knows when his chain is being jerked, and lets him jerk it.

"You went back to the scene of the *crying*," the Shoemaker says.

"You're a cruel man, a frighteningly cruel man."

"And you're a weak nobody, Mister Lonely, a pathetically weak nothing."

"Same thing."

"It seems that way, doesn't it, *finocchio*[9]?"

Then Lonely talks quickly, improvising for freedom's sake. He wants to get out alive. He thinks he has found the Shoemaker's Achilles heel: jealousy. He presses there.

"I ran into her with this *guy* next at a gas station near where it happened," Lonely says. "I reached inside my pocket for a book of matches and nearly lit the flame that would blow him straight down to hell and kingdom come, but I thought better of it. I said to myself: *Revenge is best served cold, not hot.*"

"What's his name?"

"*Duncan.*"

"Spell it," the Shoemaker says.

"D-U-N-C-A-N. Do you know him?"

"I know everybody. He may be your ticket out of here. Now, get back to this Duncan."

"I saw Simone meet Duncan for his lunch break. I turned away when that brute kissed this angel full on the mouth and left smudges and fingerprints on her face. It made me sick."

8   Curse your dead relatives.

9   Fairy

"At first, I thought you were in it only for kicks," the Shoemaker says, "but now I see you're just a dreamer. This shop, for instance."

"What about it?"

"You think you'll open it?"

"Why not? Just waiting for approval. What do you know about it?"

"It won't pass. What's it zoned for?"

"A shoemaker shop, you know damn well."

"I do. Fought hard for it. The past has got a chokehold on the present. But look at this place: mirror on the wall, a chair, no, two, counter, espresso maker, combs, brushes, capes. Does this prove you're not going to *disturb its original use?*"

"Should," says Lonely.

"They're bureaucrats. They act according to laws and bylaws. You might know the snafu, but you don't know the snag."

"What's the snag?"

"The past," the Shoemaker says. "The past has got a dead hand. It chokes out the present and keeps the future in a tight grip. A gag order, issued by the past, is still in effect. From the last will and testament of time, your inheritance is: 'And you, shut your mouth.' Closest to the truth, silence is time's decree. So it goes with time, so it goes with me. You can't win."

Lonely wants out. So, he decides to mess with his interrogator. Implicate somebody else: *Duncan.* Betray somebody you don't know. Insane jealousy will likely do the rest. Lonely makes his move.

"My revenge consisted of knowing that she could be mine, if I played my cards right. I won, don't you see. I took her away from Duncan. She was mine. And *that*, my vicious friend, is the story of how I *got* Simone. But she didn't fight for me. So, she's *free*. She's *yesterday*."

"Don't posture up. Don't dare stand up to me. Don't look at me."

The Shoemaker sobs, feeling the weight of somebody getting the better of him and besting him. He has the wrong guy and knows it. He will get around to Duncan soon enough and fix him.

"Now, I think I'm going for dinner," Lonely says, daring to leave, "table for *one*."

He breaks away, collects his things, picks up the Shoemaker's keys, and just walks out. It is enough. It is that easy. The Shoemaker goes to the window, draws aside the curtain and gestures to the Shadows to let Lonely pass. Breezing by his captors, Lonely walks away from *The Lonely Barber*, and heads north on Clinton.

The Shoemaker gives two, long, loud blasts of the whistle. He switches off the overhead lights, sits in the dark in the barber chair, frowns and fans out his deck of cards. Then lets the deck fly directly at the door into the faces of three assailants now bursting in. Identified as Simone Rebello (the hostage), Elena D'Amico (the hostage-taker) and Falconeri, the Falcon (the driver), they have pulled up to *The Lonely Barber* Shop. The Fleetwood Cadillac is rocking with sound, beats, and bass. They surprise two goon-shaped shadows hanging outside the place, waiting, eating paninis. Their firepower outguns them. The Shadows scurry off to intimidate again another day. On their way in, the trio bursts open the door, and, in the darkness, overwhelms the Shoemaker.

"*Ciao, Nonno*, you dirty bastard," Elena says.

"Elena," he chokes, "*figlia di putana*."

"This is my grandfather," she says to Simone. "Trying to recapture his youth, keeping a tight grip on the neighbourhood, and cheating on my Nonna, right, Nonno?

"Don't Nonno me," he says. "You bring them here, wielding weapons. Simone, you lying, cheating *putana, troia*[10], just wait, and Falconeri, they're going to serve you up in kidney bean soup when I'm done with you."

"I got a recipe for it, but make it *pasta e fagioli, past'e'fazzu*," the Falcon says, once a cook always a cook. "*I tiempi: na voto e mò.*[11] Past and present."

In the dark, the Falcon bullies the old man until he is forced to sit still in the barber chair. Elena throws a black cape around him, tight around the neck. Then orders *Simone* to shave the *customer*. When she refuses, Elena begins lathering the old man's face herself and goes for the straight razor lying on the counter. The Falcon and Simone hold the handguns, more on each other than the old man.

"You'll cut his throat," Simone says. "Let me do it."

"You'll cut my throat," he says. "Let *her* do it. Family is family."

The Falcon enjoys watching the shave. He is taping it with his cellphone. Elena wipes off her grandfather's face. Splashes an abrasive on his wet cheeks, slapping him and clapping her hands close to his

10   Whore

11   The times: then and now, past and present.

nose.

"I'll be shitting blood if I sit in this chair much longer," he says, "I've got piles."

So, he is hemmorhoidal. It shouldn't be funny, but it is. It's a bad day to bleed.

"A bloodletting is good for you," says the Falcon, "especially in a barber chair."

He's not exactly thinking about barber-surgeons of the past, but the effect is the same. The Falcon claps him on the back.

"Don't touch me," the Shoemaker says.

"Who wants to?" the Falcon asks, recoiling in a mock gesture of disgust.

"Do me a favour, Falconieri," the Shoemaker says.

"What is it?"

"*Vaffanculo.*"

"Right here," the Falcon says, slapping his own ass. "Be careful, or one day, they'll hang you upside down, like a cured prosciutto. That's what happens to *dictators.*"

"You can't lay a finger on me," the Shoemaker says, "let alone get rid of me."

"No, I'll be the one cutting you into thin slices and serving you up with cantaloupe melon at Italian weddings."

"*Stronzolo, imbecile, figlio di putana,*" the Shoemaker says.

"Name calling from such a filthy mouth," the Falcon says, "but leave my mother out of this. Everything you think is shit. Everything you say is shit. Everything you do is shit. And you call me *a piece of shit, an idiot* and *a bastard.* You're just a tyrannical toad. Why are you so angry?"

"I don't know," the Shoemaker says. "Never mind that."

"Here's a piece of advice: *Don't die angry.*"

"You're afraid of me," the Shoemaker says.

"I'm afraid of your breath," the Falcon says.

Simone laughs, despite herself. It has something to do with the way the Falcon is *messing* with the Shoemaker. It's good to bait him, but better to best him.

"What are you going to do to me?" the Shoemaker asks his granddaughter.

"Give him *this*," Elena says.

The *letter* from City Hall, passing from one to another, is handed to him.

"They won't let him open this shop," Simone says.

"He's the loneliest barber in the city," the Shoemaker says. "The City won't approve the application. He's finished here."

"You did it to him," the Falcon says. "Take off your shoes."

"I'm a better businessman than he is," the Shoemaker says.

"Walk out of here while you still can," Elena says, "but barefoot, old man."

"Business is business," he says, removing his shoes. "In business, he's a born loser. But your man is not here."

"Where is he?"

"Went for dinner, I think. I *let* him go. I got my sights on somebody else. What's this got to do with you anyway? How do you know him?"

"Never mind. I'll tell you later, or you'll find out. I'm just doing the job you couldn't do. Where's Lonely?"

"The Café," the Falcon suggests, but fears she wants the barber back.

"Hell, let's go, I'll finish him off myself," Elena says, or they think that's what she says.

Once the Falcon throws the Shoemaker's shoes at him, he and Simone chase after Elena in her fury. From the abandoned shop, the Shoemaker can be heard uttering curses, but he is forced to realize that his breath smells like feet.

PART TWO

1. LONELY NO MORE

F ree. Free to flee the scene of the *crying,* or the *crime.* Free again, everybody guesses, from the hostile light of confinement to the delicately branching pattern of spreading twilight, and doing his best to leave the beating and interrogation behind. Elena can just picture him escaping from the Shoemaker and his revenge games. But Lonely is not picturing her at all. He's free to think of anything else but her and the past. Freedom has its desire, its cry, and its blood. It also has its scent, its stink. It smells like victory or defeat. On Clinton Street, freedom has the smell of pizza coming from Bitondo's Pizzeria, and hot veal and roasted peppers on a bun coming from San Francesco's Food. Yet Lonely is heading for the Café Del Pop for the aroma of a double espresso short. It smells of the kind of freedom he is after. He has escaped, for the time being.

Freedom also smells like beer, as it does when Lonely passes by the Monarch Tavern on his way to the Café at the corner of Clinton and College. The Lonely Barber has made it to the Café and is now ordering. His usual waitress, Elena, isn't there. Where the hell is she? This will give him a moment of jasmine-scented peace.

"I'm Marta," the new server says, waiting on his table. "I'll be your waitress."

"Where's Elena?" he asks.

She tells him they haven't seen her all day. She is nowhere to be found. The regular cook is missing too. The Falcon is gone. But the others in the Café recognize Lonely. He has a place here, an identity. A sound beats inside him now, a word, a name, raw to the bone, his real name: *Jude.* He orders a double espresso short and a calzone. Then takes out a stubby pencil and scribbles a note on a paper serviette he intends to send to Simone. The note reads: *Lonely No More.* He signs it: *Jude.* Or he will just text her later; the kiss-off is colder that way. He is thinking about the shop. But what does he want with the barbering, anyway? He wants what the Shoemaker brags about, especially in his day, is that it? He is fighting against him, battling the past. The past owns the future. The battleground is the here-and-now. Barbering will help him simplify things. And where will that get him? He doesn't want to be Lonely anymore.

"What's your name, honey?" Marta asks, serving him.

"I'm Jude," he says. "I'm *Jude*. You Italian?"

"Polish, but I'm partial to Italians," she says.

"Sometimes, I'm partial to Polish girls," he says, feeling the freedom of saying it.

"Italians never stop surprising me," Marta says.

"Full of surprises, but I'm only half."

"The good-looking half," she says. "Say, did you hear about this Italian guy, Renato *something*, died this week?"

"No," he says.

"His kids honoured him in their own way. He was in the coffee pot business, you know, the eight-sided Moka. They cremated their papa and put his ashes in the pot. Their pop created the thing, and now he's buried in it. It's all over the Italian-speaking world—millions of pots, minus one. The dead man ran the company. What a tribute. At the funeral mass, the priest is there, and so is the deceased *in a coffeemaker*. It's in the family tomb, in case his wife wakes up, like Juliet, and needs to make an espresso. Her husband's ashes make a fine blend."

"That's how it goes when we're dead," he says. "Best not to talk about death."

"You're right. Spoils the appetite. I hear they call you Lonely."

"Because of my shop, *The Lonely Barber*, on Clinton, if the City approves."

"A barber."

"I'm still waiting," he scoffs, putting his hand into his pocket to fondle the straight razor.

She goes off to serve another customer. There it is now: a day like this with its unforgettable blows, the revenge game, the stories just to survive. You have to be resilient. That bastard, d'Arborio, *swollen Mussolini of the Soul*,[12] still has a stranglehold on the shop. So it goes in the city.

So he thinks it over: what is it that makes him want to stick it out with scissors and hair, anyway? He isn't a barber on Penny Lane, as in the song by the Beatles, but every head he has the *pleasure* to know usually complains about the city. He likes the dialogue, cutting hair and gabbing with the clients. Some are concerned about the changes to the bylaws, or the influx of refugees, or the gun violence, or the stolen bikes. Others grumble about the disappointing showing of the Maple Leafs, the hockey team, losing year in and year out, and the Raptors, the basketball team, and even the Blue Jays, the baseball team, all come in for verbal slagging. For still others, there is general outrage that the city is undergoing gentrification, or not undergoing it fast enough. What about the bike thieves, and this guy named Igor Kenk? He wants his city back, so he steals thousands of bikes. Every hair on every head has something to say about city life. Every scissor action keeps in time with the talk. Yet he stays focused on the haircut and on their cutting words. They are talking wounds. Mouths express the suffering of living here. They are no longer just words and idle chitchat. They've become an infestation of criticisms crawling on their hair, like lice, or creeping up out of the depths of their wounded mouths. *Itchy-bitchy,* he thinks, *itchy-bitchy.* As long as he can cut their hair, he will help to scratch. Are any hipsters happy being where they are? Is the city made up of malcontents? They itch and bitch about the time of garbage pickup and the noise of the garbage trucks, the raccoons, and the dumpster divers early in the morning, the honking horns at traffic lights, the despair of motorists that they might not make the advance left turn at St. Clair and Spadina. Monday morning comes too soon to the city for their liking. Insane parking officers give out traffic tickets with nothing better to do than issue tickets and target innocent people. Tow truck companies are in cahoots with the meter maids. How long does anyone have to park on Yonge Street? How long do lights stay green on the major thoroughfares? Have they not outlawed squeegee kids? They pour their shitty water on the windshields even when the drivers wave them off. How many pedestrians will be run down this year? Eighteen in one day, is that a record? Why do pedestrians on Bloor not use the lights just feet away from where they want to cross? All exit signs and parking signs are confusing, maybe, deliberately so. Lonely joins in quoting clients and their list of complaints, their lamentations about living in the city: *This city is very quickly going nowhere.* They are urban stories that he likes because they are part of his own dreamed-up city. For these complaints, and for the way he deals with them while working for other barbers cutting hair, Jude (a. k a. the Lonely Barber) gets great tips. He concludes that it is about *Scissors & Hair*. But what happens if the dream dies?

Isn't it strange how the waitress, Marta, has been talking about death and dying while he is trying to eat? Will she put ashes in his espresso? The coffeemaker is an urn. They will honour your last wishes, or they won't. When he dies, will his remains be swept up with the hair from a barbershop floor, or flushed down the drain by some shampoo girl? "The more you eat, the more you die," his father likes to say, thinking of dying himself from a self-inflicted wound. Still, the mention of death on a day like this with its memorable blows, you have to endure them to make it in the city, and in life. City life lets the dead bury the dead. Toronto has many cemeteries and burial grounds. The citizens are walking on bones and shells. Superstitions die hard, especially when he is expecting news. So the mention of death is not so good when he is waiting for the letter on a dead letter day. When will it come? Will City Hall kill his dream? They say they'll send him their decision by snail mail, not by email. Which address do they have? Do they have the wrong one? He has also sent many emails, has called, even visited. The secretary of the department, Marianne, flirts with him, reassures him, these things take time, right, right. She's not lying, is she, and playing with him? He has invested so much in the shop, has provided sketches of the interior, and has shown that there will be no structural changes. Shoemaker's shop to barbershop is an easy transition. That tyrant, d'Arborio, thinks he owns it, not outright, but in the legal wrangle, red tape from a tangle of days gone by. In perpetuity, he keeps saying. Amen. Isn't that the gist of the kidnapping and interrogation? The City can be kind to refugees, immigrants, and street people. It welcomes artists, stars, writers, filmmakers, dreamers, migrants, drifters and business people alike. Or it can be cruel to them all. A bad review and your play or film is a flop. The critics carry their own whips and pack their own six-shooters. A deal gone bad or wrong and you can be buried on the spot. Why be cruel to a barber or any trade? "Let me open my shop," he thinks. What can possibly prevent it? What address has he given them?

Marta brings him his order, and stands by just looking at him.

"Enjoy," she says, smiling.

Jude can, will and does. She leaves him alone, but returns quickly. Then pulls out a letter, slides it across the table with the tips of her long, thin fingers towards his hand, and touches him.

"What's this?"

"This just came for you."

"Here?"

"Special delivery. I think you already know the messenger. Just look what the hellcat dragged in."

Jude swings around. Elena is standing in the doorway. She struts into the Café and sways to his table, clicking her heels, pulling Simone by the wrist. What's with the swagger?

"Don't shoot the messenger," Simone says.

"You gave them my address when we were living together," Elena says.

"You opened it," he says. "You opened my mail. No respect."

"It came for you, while you were away, after you dumped me. No forwarding address. Bad news. No shop. I hope it hurts."

"Revenge is best served by a jealous *waitress*," the Falcon says from the doorway, "especially if you've slept with her and dumped her."

Jude reads the letter. With rules and regulations, zoning laws and bylaws, old laws put a rear, naked choke on both the present and future. In that location, you can open a shoemaker shop, but *not* a barbershop.

"Look," Elena says. "It's a blow. It hurts, right?"

"We call it the Heartbreaker Sandwich," the Falcon blurts out.

"It hurts like hell, *but*," Simone says.

"Just as well," Jude thinks. He sips his coffee. "Let me finish my dinner."

"Do you want me to stay with you?" asks Elena before Simone can.

"Tonight, I eat *alone*," he says, rejecting them both.

It is like dumping Elena twice. She turns tail and takes off. The Falcon, waiting for her and Simone, puts his wing-like arms around them, and off they fly.

Marta brings him another espresso. A note on the saucer reads: "If you're *lonely* again, call me." Her number is on the back.

"Let's hook up," she says. "I'm a good listener, a good shoulder to cry on, or lie on."

She smiles over her right shoulder and leaves him alone. Not lonely, he thinks, but alone. The lone barber. He needs time to get it together. Then again, why not just move on? He has to find his place in the city, but first it has to be re-imagined. This is what he tells Marta later that night, early morning really, once he has called her, gone up to her place, an apartment in the Annex, and, after they have talked and talked and finished drinking wine and coffee, kissed, gone to bed, Jude decides to move in. He is always moving in and out. It is a prelude to moving on. End of a bad romance can be the start of something else. By romancing the Six, maybe he and Marta can find their bliss together in a re-imagined city. Why dream alone? Here or elsewhere, beyond the city limits, if the city receives love, but refuses to love them back, it has to be mutual, requited, between you and your city.

When Jude mentions his debts, Marta says, "Pay them down. Pay them off."

She has cash, not just from tips. The waiting on tables is for the fun of it. She has savings. She is also between dreams. Jude is her *half-Italian* fun for now. She wants to see what will happen next. There is a certain kind of fun that needs money. Funds it. Besides, he can pay her back, once he opens his *new* shop with her help. If he can't pay, she can and will, and next day, Marta does. Nobody, especially Elena, counts on that. Marta has a car, a Karmann Ghia, just like the one Jude's father has always wanted. They drive down to College and Clinton past the Café Del Popolo and scoot down and take a quick and free look at *The Lonely Barber*. He doesn't feel like going in, if she doesn't mind, or else he would show her the interior. Instead, they decide to take a trip to some of the other towns and cities that might be right for a new business venture, a small barbershop, one chair, one barber, with maybe a business manager, someone to take appointments, make the coffee, sweep up hair, someone to sleep with the barber when the day is done. *Marta.* Or they will feel the gravitational and elastic pull back to their neighborhood. They have to check it out. He has never thought of having a partner before. Even still, how does it get there so fast: chaos to cooperation? Still-evolving. She is kind, too kind. He cuts her hair, styles it, the New York hairdo, just two snips, and let the remaining hair fall where it will. Marta loves it. They laugh until the sun comes up. He is about to go, but she presses him to stay. It happens suddenly. She is quick in her generosity. Imagine if partners such as Marta don't exist. To leave the city, they head east through the villages and districts of T.O. (the Distillery District, Leslieville, the Beaches) and head up the Don Valley to the 401, Highway of Heroes. Next stop, anywhere, but here. All at once, they put the visors down for shade against the rising sun.

Behind them, the Falcon, Simone (along for the predatory ride) and Elena are in pursuit. The Falcon is putting her wise, saying that Lonely has dumped her twice. She wants to swoop down on the escapees. She has something to *say* to Lonely, and something to *do* to his new Boo, Marta. The Falcon says they are city-born birds and won't fly far.

"But he keeps dumping you. Let's let him go and get back."

He keeps trying to tell Elena, despite the cruelty, that love dies. So let it. Why chase after Lonely? Let him go. Let him be. That is Simone's opinion, too, ever since the message she receives from Lonely spells out a tearless goodbye for not standing by, a kiss-off after what he has heard or figured out, and simply lets love die, even before it starts. The Falcon puts his wing-like arm around Simone's shoulder. They have become close. Closer since he removes the handcuffs, drives her away from d'Arborio and his shadowy crew, and fixes her a midnight meal, the real deal, the heavenly hash, a decadent dish, Simone's favorite, chocolate cake. A tall glass of milk and getting her gun back are all it takes to free her from the bonds of the last day and any residual resentment that may still be attached to the events. She has dreamed it out loud. No police for what has been done to her. She has also done things and has a past. Besides, you only call the police if you live in Forest Hill or Scarborough. But she lives in Little Italy, she jokes, so no police.

Elena bites into the Falcon's face, insisting that he drive them in pursuit of the Karmann Ghia. She has staked out Marta's place and watches them takeoff. When they head down to Little Italy, she believes that she can trap them with her grandfather's help and muscle, but they escape, flee past the shop and travel east along College. Elena hates to do it, but she has to get to the East end of the city and beyond. If need be, she'll even go past Victoria Park, something she normally doesn't like to do.

"All right, all right," the Falcon says, once he has been bitten into. "What's your ride, little lady, the pride of the streets, my pimped-out Van, or the luxury insides of the Fleetwood Caddy?"

"I want a Karmann Ghia, like hers," Elena says.

"No can do," he says. "Could do once, but those days are gone, no more jacking cars. I say no to German engineering, with an unsavory past, crimes *against,* sounds like a seized-up lawnmower, you can hear it coming, not humming, miles and miles away. For miles and miles, we'll chase and catch them, but let it be a Black, Pimped-Out Van or the blood-red Caddy."

"Or better still," Simone says. "Let's take my Fiat 500 Pop."

"Intimate," the Falcon says. "Patriotic. *A Saturday-Night Special* with a tiny perfect bullet for the hit, I get it, let's get it, get in and get out and get it on and get it right. Let's get. I'll bring my mix-tape, or rap and do hip-hop live for the little ladies."

The Canary Yellow Fiat 500 Pop speeds out of the city, not knowing where to go, or how to get there. The chase is the point, and the thrill of the chase pleases the Falcon and Simone in the front seats. But Elena, cramped and rammed into the backseat, chewing on the headrest, just wants Lonely back.

"What to do for money?" the Falcon asks. "Who is bankrolling this pursuit, to keep me in the kind of Mustard-coloured jackets and black shirts and tight pants and pointy shoes I'm accustomed to?"

Elena has cash on her and money in the bank. She has her credit cards and bankcards. Simone has been compensated for her "companionship." She has served her time with the Shoemaker. He has paid for her university education. She has been his *sugar baby,* and he, her ex-sugar daddy. He has paid for at least 70 young women to help finish their schooling, textbooks, tuition, and rent. It is *sugaring* for them. For him, it is a succession of sweet companions in his retirement, his declining and reclining years. His wisdom and business acumen are worthy of the restaurants, shows and motels he takes them to. But the sugar daddy is not wanted on this voyage. He has to make more calls at the U. of T. or York University for another sweet companion. Simone, his ex-sugar baby, is leaving him for good. She has all the taxable income she needs for the time being, and she has the Falcon to buy things for, and keep him in yellow and black, and keep him from getting sad from the world news, and keep him rapping and rhyming. Between them, Simone and Elena have enough money, more than the Falcon can burn through on the chase.

"Beyond the Six is not the end of the world, but you can see it from there," he says.

"Fly," Elena commands, driven to get Lonely back. "Fly."

The Falcon, unhooded, like a soaring bird at a falconer's flight command, wants to do just that. If only. He wants to lift his flashy-red, long-winged 1959 Fleetwood Caddy's front end on its hopping, hydraulic suspension, and fly after Lonely and his new Boo, Marta—0 to 60 in 10 flat. But they aren't in the Cadillac. Instead, they pile into Simone's canary-yellow Fiat 500 Pop. She lets them persuade her to speed. She is behind the wheel, and like a little, yellow bird, the Fiat 500 Pop flies 0—60 in 9.4 seconds flat.

Stuck behind the shadow of a belling, eastbound streetcar on College, spinning sparks, and loading the air with ghosts of blue electricity, a block in back of the Fiat 500 Pop and two from the Karmann Ghia, a black Hummer, like a huge black bug, is bearing down on both vehicles, looking to *bring it*. Like Elena, her grandfather won't give up, and neither will his Shadows.

On and on, so it goes in the city, and so it goes in mad love, mutual or unrequited, jealous or giving, even in the pangs of despised love. A perpetual car chase will likely end in a car crash with the Jaws of Life extracting lovers and other drivers from a multi-vehicle pileup. But Jude and Marta are simply moving on.

2. TORONTO AGAINST EVERYBODY

Beyond cruising speed, the Falcon talks about what he'll likely miss most if leaving the city for good. The cafés, the Entertainment District, and other areas come to mind, China Town, the Distillery District, College Street, Bloor Street West, the Bay and Gable Houses in Little Italy, Christie Pits and a ballgame on a summer night.

The Falcon keeps looking left and right, passing through the small towns: Pickering, Ajax, Whitby. He is confident that he has eluded the Hummer, for the time being, and likely leaving that enormous black bug in a multi-vehicle pile-up on the 401, or lost in the tangled net of the east end. He says that Toronto has its gravitational pull and determines who gets to leave and who must remain.

"Toronto against *Everybody*, every town and city," the Falcon says. "Yeah, right, we called in the Army to shovel our snow. You laugh at us. You hate us and still call us Muddy York and Hog Town. You hate us for our colours, our raccoons, our Wellesley and Jarvis, our street festivals, our Maple Leafs."

They miss Little Italy and the city already some 30 miles and 45 minutes away. On the lookout for Lonely's hometown (that's where Elena guesses he is going), the Falcon is killing himself laughing. His cheeks hurt, saying: "*Osh-awa, the Shwa, Osh-awa, the Shwa.*"

"The Toronto-haters hate the same things, that's all you ever hear: pollution, noise, crazy drivers, crazies at Bathurst and St. Clair, traffic, honking, the cost of living, too expensive, garbage, rats, raccoons, street meat, refugees, ugly Rita, the Meter Maid, aggressively carrying out her duties on Bloor Street. And those that like us all like the same things: the trees, city in a forest, diversity, cultural stuff, art galleries, music, High Park, green spaces, street music, the beaches, free stuff, Kensington Market, Honest Ed's, the ROM, but not the Crystal, shows and job opportunities."

"What would you miss if it all went missing?" asks Simone.

"Man, right now, staring at the semis and the fields and the hawks, I'm missing the Danforth," says the Falcon.

"Why the Danforth?"

"Greek Town, man, the restaurants, the street festival," he says, then lets the beat of his desire overtake him. "Look at that, the birds up in the sky. I'm thinking of our city birds, especially by the waterfront and the Island. Hard to forget over the rigging, our city-born birds escape nets of wide-flung light and soar above Ontario Place. Witnesses of their flight's winged geometry still wonder at their crystal-clear call and cry. An artist can capture their easy flight, *firm as birds' wings, but a frayed embrace.* Once, on the Centre Island Loop, giving in to daybreak, a lone side-wheeler ferryboat blasted a loud good morning to *me*. From the Trillium's cracked bell, a lone falcon (not me, but the other bird) soared above Golden weeping willows, honey locusts and cottonwoods. Ground bass of water music muscles in with the lake's early morning soundings. Ferried to Hanlan's Point, or Mugg's Island or Algonquin is the pleasure of the place. Fully aware of my stare, the captured city surrenders to my glare. Let's go back."

More beat-box, but then the backseat starts bouncing.

"What are you doing?" Elena asks him.

"Keeping a lookout for the exit to your ex's hometown," the Falcon says, messing with Elena. "So you can lunge into *the* Shwa, the *Shwa*, and stick it to him. But he keeps dumping you. Let's let him go and get back."

The Falcon is amusing his accomplishes with talk of Lady Balls, thanks to a radio ad. He is saying how we are all women and we are all men, and that there is only a distinction with indoor and outdoor plumbing.

"Balls are balls, as we know them," he says.

"So grow a pair," Elena blurts out. "Or let them drop."

"But women have balls, too, called ovaries," he says, giving an anatomy lesson.

He insists that his companions are well endowed with Lady Balls. The whole pursuit is ballsy, no matter how they are hanging and where they are situated. Simone, popping gingersnaps to ward off carsickness, agrees that she has the kind of balls he is referring to, no disrespect intended to those battling ovarian cancer, for that is the point of the ad, but Elena doesn't want to hear the word *balls* in connection with ovaries. At least, not the connection they are making in the front seat. She has brothers, and, of course, her father and grandfather, and uncles and male cousins who seem particularly fond of balls, touching them, hefting them, grabbing each others', and bringing them up in every conversation and situation. That is what she has always liked about

Lonely, who although he has a pair, doesn't seem as obsessed with his as much as other guys. Pocket pool makes her sick. They're always humming and touching themselves. But the farther away from the city they get with farmland on both sides of the highway, the more this kind of talk doesn't really work. There's an Urban Dictionary for Urban Slang. Are there a *Suburban Word List* and *Approved Topics* for those who are not urban saints or hipsters?

"We're going to have to figure where he'd go," Simone says.

"The Shwa," Elena says, decisively. "I already told you."

"Ottawa?"

"Oshawa."

"Sounds Japanese."

"It's not the end of the world, but you can see it from there," the Falcon says. "Wayne and Shuster, of blessed memory, said so on TV. Why would Lonely go there?"

"He used to talk about the factory town where he grew up."

"And you think he's going home? Maybe, set up a shop. Get away from Toronto."

"Maybe," Simone says, now sipping ginger ale (Schweppes). "Family, maybe."

"The Shwa it is," says the Falcon, growing a pair. "Tell me when we get there. I might pass through without knowing it and fall off the edge of the world."

"That noise, that noise, pipe down," Elena says.

"I think we got a flat tire," the Falcon says.

It is then Elena gives him a swift cuff and a convincing slap across the back of his raven-haired head.

She gets out to fix the flat, crazy to get back to the car chase. The Falcon is filming her with his cellphone. When she lifts her short skirt to use the tire iron on the lug nuts, he rolls down the window and shouts over the truckers' horns:

"That's the money shot."

"*Mamaluke*[13]," Elena says, and gives his ogle eyes another point of view.

13
male
          Italian-American slang putting down a stupid

3. URBAN LEGENDS

In the Karmann Ghia, the farther they get from the Six, the more Jude is telling Marta about his experiences in the city. How somebody keeps keying his Jeep Liberty, not once or twice, but three or four times, because he tries to park it on the street, and is taking some vengeful, brainless bastard's spot.

"I waited for him, but never caught him," Jude says. "He remains nameless, faceless, hiding behind his cruelty. My father said it was time to get out of the city."

Marta recounts how the toilet keeps backing up from the upstairs' tenant flushing pads or fabric softeners. There is shit floating in her sink, and a flotilla of shit sailing in her backed-up tub. The filth is all over the floor. The landlord has the pipes reamed out from time to time, but since it keeps happening, she finally decides to move out.

Jude goes on about raccoons, dumpster divers, endless taxicabs, honking horns, shootings in the Eaton's Centre, and the *Summer of the Gun*. It is enough to make anybody want to leave. Is this why the rest of the country hates Toronto? Maybe, it is best to settle in a small town. A university town, he concludes, but will it be open to the idea of a big-city barber settling in their community? He will likely bring urban savvy to the place. Durham Region has colleges, a university. Peterborough is a university town. Kingston, for sure, has Queens University, and even Belleville has its college. No more fighting the traffic, putting up with panhandlers, rats and raccoons, blood, puke and smashed watermelons in the streets on Sunday mornings after *howlings* and Saturday night brawls. Maybe, Toronto is an idea whose time has come, and that time is past. There are reasons to go, but also reasons to stay.

But Marta, while agreeing in principle, and while accepting his view to be kind, starts presenting her own views. It is the psycho-geography of urban living, and so she links the idea of landscape/cityscape and mind. Marta suggests imagining and re-imagining the city. She speaks about personal stories and civic history. She speaks about the spring festival of city-dwelling bike riders: the "Blessing of the Bikes" at Trinity-St. Paul's Centre. She says she has taken part in the Spring Spiritual Tune-up, and insists everybody should.

Jude says: "What's going on? Have they found a new constellation in the sky called *the Cyclist?*"[14]

He says that he, too, likes to ride his Bianchi through the city. He loves his bike.

"Bless the riders," he says, "and their rides."

And he says how much it breaks his heart to see ghost bikes, festooned with plastic flowers, especially for a little kid's bike. Marta says it is time to take back the streets.

"Let's rethink the city," Marta says, "and ways of finding our bliss or happiness in a happy city."

She speaks about the city's imagination, and, therefore, its pulse, vitality and rare beauty. They talk about the city planners and the legal hassles, and the legalized crooks, and those that will break your heart and stomp on your dreams, if you don't have a license. They talk of visionaries like the one behind Casa Loma, building it for his wife, but then bureaucrats outwit him, and steal his dream.

"That dream belongs to everybody now," Marta says, "and they're even performing same-sex marriages at Casa Loma."

East of the Six, Jude takes the off-ramp to his hometown. It isn't the end of the world, but you can see it from there. That old joke: he laughs at the laugh.

"Everybody that loves the city that *motovates* Canada loves small towns," Jude says, "the lake view, proximity to Toronto, and relative safety. The haters hate the downtown for not being trendy enough. They also dislike the trashers."

They turn down a side street, and then left onto Centre Street. When they make a right onto Gibb Street, they see a sign in the window of a house on the corner. The sign reads: *Welcome to the Shwa. She's dirty, but it's home.*

"Civic pride," Marta says. "A joke, but the place doesn't look dirty at all."

"Or no pride," Jude says. "When is funny just not funny."

They make a right on Nassau Street and another right onto John Street, past Memorial Park with the Band Shell and the bronze soldiers standing on guard, and back onto Simcoe Street. When they park the Karmann Ghia, they find themselves downtown by the Methadone Clinic near the Four Corners at King and Simcoe. A slight movement of their heads and they take in the Post Office, Fazio's Restaurant, the bank, one of many in their surround view. Churches, too, one with a spire, four corners and four churches close by, clustered, aspiring skyward.

A homeless man stands guard outside the TD bank. The place has money. He has none. He is wearing too many coats for the season, and totes far too many bags. He keeps his balance by anchoring himself to the sidewalk, tilting his head back and bellowing. He wants something from his city. It isn't too hard to figure out what. Jude has seen him before on other visits to his hometown, before he stops coming back altogether.

"He's ripening here," he says, "maturing, rotting."

"You know him?" asks Marta.

"I call him Grisly Adams, hairy, big as a dancing bear."

Grisly begins growling at him. Jude pulls out his snips from his leather bag. He is not about to give him his few remaining coins.

"I'm gonna cut you," he says. "Snip, snip, shear you and trim you till you're back to clean-cut and clean-shaven."

"Knife me, do me a favour," the Bear growls. "Cut my throat, man."

"Your hair and beard," Marta says. "A trim. I can get you a coffee, if you like, and a muffin."

"There's a Tim's[15] around the corner," Jude says.

"Just a coffee," the talking Bear says. "I can get a muffin anytime at the Salvation Army."

"That's just down the road, past the park," Jude says. "Now, what about that haircut?"

They go to the donut shop. The Bear, lumbering, follows. Marta walks in for the coffees. But when the Bear refuses to go in, Jude starts cutting his hair, standing, dancing around him, and trims his beard. The thing of it is, the Bear stands, unmoving, holding his bags, sweating in the heat, eyes glazed with tears.

Simone gives him his coffee, a *Double-Double*, with "Roll-up-the-rim-to-win," and says how young he looks, shaven and shorn. Grisly keeps crying. He knows he's not going to win. The waterworks erode the dirt on his face, like tiny rivers across arid land. But he no longer looks hard, and less bearlike. He walks away, goes back to his station in front of the bank, turns to stone.

15   Tim Horton's donut shop

"I think his real name is Joshua."

"Joshua of Oshawa."

Jude takes Marta to Memorial Park for a picnic. In the Band Shell, a band is playing dance tunes from the past. They dance on the grass near the Cenotaph, a war memorial for the dead. Jude buys Marta an ice cream from the Dickie Dee on a bike. They kiss under a chestnut tree, walk down to the flats and under the bridge, along the creek, cross the footbridge, and then head back downtown. The aim is clear: to find a good place to set up a barbershop. They go looking for a motel or a hotel to stay the night, talk it over, make a quick, sexy decision, go back, stay, or move on, but first they have to sleep on it. Motel Six is as good a place as any for an unplanned *honeymoon in the Shwa*. It is sex in a small town motel, like in the movies. They are dreaming out loud, dreaming together.

Fixing the flat on the side of the highway, Elena can just picture it.

"Yeah, right," she says over the noise of highway traffic, twisting the lug nuts this way and that, "but what about *me*? Spoiler alert: I've seen this movie before. In this flick, there's a chick with a mustache, skirt hiked up to her waist, changing a tire on the side of the highway. You make her bleed, dump her twice, and she's supposed to lump it. But on your trail, she's riding your tail, in more than a jealous mood. She carries a secret in her belly that will soon start to show, and mess with your plans. If hips don't lie, what about a baby bump? And who put it there? *You. You did, the guy once known as the Lonely Barber. You got one past the goalie. He shoots, he scores, the Falcon would say, if he knew. Who was the goalie? Not Simone or Marta, but me, the waitress in mad love—Elena D'Amico.*"

So, she won't let the movie end there, if she can help it, not without another plot twist, or at least a good reaction shot.

Elena has been waving off truckers who want to lend a helping hand, especially when she bends over. No thanks. You can never tell what's going to happen so far away from home.

"Let's roll," she says, the flat fixed, and the Fiat 500 Pop rolls, looking for the Shwa, and lurching towards Jude's hometown.

4. THE CITY THAT *MOTOVATES* CANADA

"This is some kind of sign," says the Falcon.

"What kind of sign?"

"The flat," he says, "and the sight of your magnificent butt, but maybe we shouldn't go on."

"We're going on," Elena spits out.

"Then watching you fix the flat has made me hungry. Let's get something to eat. I know a guy at the Baker's Table at the South end of this city. Or we can turn around and get back to T.O. and I can cook up something special before we fall off the edge of the world."

"Not going back," says Elena. "I can put you on the Go-Train or a bus and you can be back in no time."

"A train, a bus? This is not just important to you; it's a violent and urgent need in your guts."

"My guts? Leave my guts out of this."

"What are you going to do when you catch up to him? Why not just let him go? He's on the run, or looking for something he can't have. The Shoemaker calls him a born loser, once a loser always a loser."

"He's gotta accept responsibility," Elena says.

"For what?" the Falcon asks. "For tasting a little of the Royal Jelly?"

"Ah, shit, you're pregnant," Simone says on a hunch. "That's why you're so intent on tracking him down."

"You're preggers?" howls the Falcon. "So take care of it, one way or the other. Or have it, then give it to me, and when it grows up, I'll tell it I'm the father."

"I could take care of it myself, but he's got to be told" insists Elena. "You can't just stay with somebody, knock them up, look away, and walk away."

"So, call him," the Falcon says. "Text him. Save on gas."

"You don't call or text that kind of news, do you?"

"So he got one past the goalie," says the Falcon. "He shoots, he scores. It's always hockey night in Canada. Sign him up for the Leafs. God knows they need a good goal scorer. Just don't become a drunken monkey wielding a butcher's knife, like I saw once in a bar in Brazil. Besides, he may already have gone back."

She hits him.

"Hey, watch the hair," he says. "And stop smacking me. What are you, my mother?"

"When you were being carsick," Elena tells Simone, "I was nauseated. But I've learned to hide it, when I can."

"You're as jealous as your Nonno," the Falcon says.

Spiteful, vengeful, yes, insanely jealous, and with green eyes, but passionate, and that is what she wants to be: alive, committed, and nobody is going to get away with cheating her, or cheating on her.

The Falcon waves at the cars and trucks honking at them, slips a CD of Italian pop tunes from the sixties into the player, accelerates on the gravelly shoulder and fishtails and speeds back onto the highway.

"Highway of Heroes," the Falcon says.

"That's what they call it."

"Highway of Heroes? All those poor, dead soldiers killed in Afghanistan, or wherever they're killing them off, for stepping on I.E.D.s, they bring them along the 401 in a hearse, coffin draped in a Canadian flag, people standing on the bridges, waving, saluting. I don't know if it's right. Would it not be better if they weren't dead?"

"They served their country."

"Ultimate sacrifice."

"Still, I'm sure their mothers would want to see them messing around, playing ball in the backyard, drinking a beer. It's just too sad. Highway of Heroes, fuck, it's best not to think about it."

He suffers the most about the world when he isn't in a kitchen cooking, or while drifting off to sleep. He says, crying:

"Wipe away the tears I cry for you. Then feed me, feed me, feed me."

5. Motel Sex

Rainy day, all day, a bottle of wine, they are lying together in Motel 6 near the highway. Marta sets out a business plan. Fair-size city, she is saying, and Jude is saying factory town, yes, but with colleges, a university, but will a trendy barbershop work here?

Marta calls the Café del Pop, checking in, and telling the owner she won't be in for her regular shift, sorry about that, something wild has come up. She doesn't know when she'll be back in Toronto, on a little vacation, and a small business venture, if it works out, points east, out Kingston-way, maybe Montreal, but back home soon, no, no plans to quit, if she doesn't have to, she likes her job, and thanks for understanding.

Jude worries a bit that it is a dream, an invention of theirs, a bad idea, a flop in the making, and waiting to happen, and how he maybe doesn't know enough about business, and doesn't know what he is doing, the rich barber and all that money talk, but still it is a business, all the old timers say so, and not a dream. It is a trade, a craft. Remember, it's a business. Keep it in mind. A business is a business. You stand on your feet all day, bent over the heads, bending your spine, talking to customers all day, and not every barber has a place in Florida and a big house, despite letting the nail grow on the little finger, and not every barber can open two shops, cutting hair day and night, and having to hear some dude say, *'Come on, buddy, blow on it, buddy, give me a good haircut,'* and tips in the tip jar, and being paid under the table, even though the tax people have it all worked out to a decimal point. How many heads do you have to cut to make ends meet?

But Marta has been in business for herself and others, she has run a company for her father, real estate, before she gets edgy about it and wants to try something different, something new (not running wild, as her father thinks and says), but maybe checking out simplifying her life, not living to make money, but making money to live, live now, the waitressing job is something to tide her over, get her to live a different kind of life, and who knows, get into music or making films, or just dancing through life.

"A different kind of life," Jude says, "if only."

That's how it is with him. Scissors and hair: it seems simple enough. No more commuting, no more pissing his time away, playing the lottery, gambling on a steady job, trying to land a secure one, like the rest of his family, and the way they do things, go to school or not, and find a job and stay there till you retire or die, whichever comes first, with money in the bank, and leave it for the kids, or piss them off and give it away to strangers. He doesn't want to disappoint Marta, the way he has disappointed others. He has Elena in mind, and Simone, but with her it ends before it even starts, and maybe himself.

"Nothing to recriminate yourself for," Marta says.

She can slip in and out of situations, always on the wing, improvising, making it up as she goes along, playing, working, and playing at work. She can pick up and leave, then pack up again, and leave off just as she feels she has to. Keep everybody guessing, even the most irresponsible and immature of friends and family.

Money, money, making it, not making it, Jude insists, spending it, not spending it, trying to save it by giving up smoking, saving it for a rainy day, and this is a rainy day, and he has no savings, rain all day, in a motel in his hometown, and thinking about what he's doing here, no money but what Marta has, no money of his own but a few coins, chasing a dream with so much cash lost, spent, and once you give it away, it won't come back. You make it yourself. Why not keep it yourself? Why not keep it for when it rains?

"It's still raining," Jude says.

"Come back to bed," Marta says, and reaches out for him.

6. Money Is Money

In the Fiat 500 Pop, they switch to the question of money. Elena keeps chanting one word: *Pimp*. But the Falcon is on a roll, and so he rolls on and on, rolling over her catcalls.

"Right, right," says the Falcon, "for those of us without cash, we're pimps. But money is money, and money is mine, as the saying goes, and you've got to make it and keep it, invest it, or get others to make it for you, and keep your money before the Taxman gobbles up every coin. I'm a cook, but I don't cook the books. I'm not saying I'm a pimp (stop calling me that), but who's buying the gas?"

Elena plucks out her Visa card.

"The plastic," she says.

"Are we going back?" asks the Falcon. "Staying on? I'm game as long as you're paying, bankrolling this chase. Where should I go now? Turn left? Turn right? There are so many one-way streets in this end-of-the-world town. This is where Lonely was born? No wonder, I'm just saying, one way, another one way, a wild goose chase, you're always back where you start from."

"What's everybody gawking at?" Simone asks. "I feel naked, everybody staring."

"Your short skirt is riding high," the Falcon says. "But it's likely the car."

"The colour?"

"That, and the freaks inside, and the make. This is General Motors country. We're driving a foreign car."

"Made by Fiat-Chrysler, right?"

"The competition."

"I don't like being ogled," Simone says, "unless it's the usual crowd."

"Toronto has its sightseers and gawkers, too," Elena says, "the male gaze is the male gaze, but."

"Freaks are freaks," says the Falcon. "You get used to the crazies."

"They think we're crazy. We think they're hicks."

They gas up and go south on Simcoe Street, and end up at the lake and Lakeview Park. Out for a stroll to stretch their legs along the lake's edge, they observe picnickers, kids at the playground, teenagers smoking dope, guys playing Frisbee, some old guy in a black speedo walking in and out of the washroom. A good idea, Simone and Elena go together, the Falcon goes into the men's.

"They've got an effing beach," the Falcon says once they wash up and saunter down to the water's edge.

"So let's get some sun, when in Rome or Oshawa, etcetera."

As Simone and the Falcon stroll on ahead to the strip of beach, Elena calls the Café in Little Italy, and gets it out of the manager that Marta has missed her shift. The manager says as far as he knows Marta is going to Kingston.

"Kingston, shit," Elena says, when she cuts him off. "What am I wasting time in the Shwa for? Where are those two?"

They are sunning themselves. The Falcon nearly throws Simone in the water. Then back into the Fiat 500 Pop (they have bought cones at the concession stand). The Falcon drives to the Baker's Table in the South end. This, that, buns, cheese, cold cuts, Brios, treats, sweets, kibitzing with the cook, Dom, and off they go.

"If I ever want to work in the Boonies, Dom offered me a job," says the Falcon.

"Where we going, anyway?"

"Kingston."

"The penitentiary?"

"Have we done this town already?" Simone asks, not really wanting a reply.

"Have they arrested your arty boyfriend?" the Falcon asks malevolently. "And don't hit me, or I'll call a cop, press charges, get the Oshawa fuzz to put you in jail. Send you in a paddy wagon to the pen in Kingston. Then you can hook up with your man, and give him the news. Slap him with a paternity suit."

She hates him, but she thinks she hates Lonely more. She hates him so much she loves him. Elena is in a rage and wants to drive.

"So drive," the Falcon says, "if you know how and the way. See what this little 500 can do, Fury 500, with a furious little pregnant woman driving. Let's get out of here. The Falcon has done the Shwa. But we're never going to find him, needle in the hay, needle in the hay, needle in the haystack."

"She's not listening," Simone says.

"She's drunk on her own hormones," the Falcon says.

He is in the back seat now, making sandwiches for the road. At least,

Elena will be pleased with what is on his mind, and what is on his mind is on the menu for the road trip to Kingston. But what is on her mind is on the mind of any bounty hunter in pursuit of the escapee.

7. From Place to Place

Jude gets a mystery call, voice sounding like a car crash, asking where Elena is, but Jude ends the call abruptly without answering. He is on the alert now and senses the bodily harm. Still, he takes Marta to meet his grandparents. They have a good visit, only sitting and sitting, till his back hurts, and they take the visit to the couch. But Marta loves meeting them.

Jude asks his grandfather if he wants a haircut. The old man laughs, running his hand over his baldhead.

"If you can find anything to cut," he says.

Then they sit in the kitchen and have tea and biscuits. The grandfather starts telling stories of the old country, including stories about cutting hair for nephews and locals that he still laughs about, and sometimes regrets. When it is time to leave, his grandfather says:

"Stay."

"We can't," Jude says. "We're on our way to Kingston."

"Stop at Cobourg," his grandmother says. "A beautiful beach there, we used to take your mom when she was a kid."

Jude says that he remembers going there himself with his mom and dad.

"We'll be sure to stop there," he says.

"Great to meet you," his grandmother says to Marta, saying goodbye.

"Don't make us miss you," Jude's grandfather says to them. "Good luck with the shop."

The old man has worked in the local factory for 35 years.

"He would rather have been a farmer and worked the land," Jude tells Marta. "But you do what you have to do, and not what you want to do. In the old days, it was duty and obligation and family, and so my grandfather made the best of it, built his own place, had a big family, still in good shape for a man in his nineties."

Today, it is different. Today, it is try this, try that. Move from place to place, occupation to occupation, but you never get it right, and you never settle.

"They seem happy," Marta says.

"Happy or unhappy, they won't change for change's sake," Jude says. "They stay still, same as it ever was, but don't ever seem bored or restless. They like things as they are in their own bungalow and backyard and basement. They got it right, I think. My grandmother is a patient person; she knows my grandfather and knows how to keep things going, steady and sure, secure in the knowledge that life is what they always thought it was, what they were taught, what their faith says it is, not what's playing on the charts, on TV, or at the movies, new experiments doomed to fail because we get bored so fast. In their own way, they got behind their dummy, or their plow, or the car part on the assembly line, or their brooms. They did what they had to do and are still doing it."

"They seem nice," Marta says. "They seem happy here."

Happy/unhappy, he isn't sure about the difference anymore. Still, he recalls his childhood and teen years, especially with his older brother and the things they get up to. The time he laughs at his brother in the pool in the backyard and gets bird shit in his open mouth. When they are older, the day they drive their dad's car and get a flat tire in the rain with the wipers broken and using his shirt to wipe the windshield. When they take it in for repairs, the shop owner wants to arm-wrestle them double or nothing for the charge. He can't remember if they went for it or not. There is always sneaking chips and pizza in the side window leading to his bedroom. He tells Marta that one day, down by the creek, they happen to find a stash of nudie mags under the bridge. One night, during a particularly nasty wrestling match, his brother throws him against a wall and he crashes through. They repair it with too much plaster and cover it with a large movie poster. Their dad finds out only twenty years later when he is forced to sell the house and the poster comes down and the story comes out. It makes Jude happy thinking about those times in his hometown, and he laughs, but a bit of sadness mixes in with the memories.

"We better move on," Jude says. "Maybe check out Kingston, as you suggested. What'd you say? We can stay over. Look around the downtown. Decide from there. Go back, or see Ottawa, Montreal, who knows? Maybe, head to the East Coast? See the Ocean?"

"Who knows?" Marta says. "Might be a stolen honeymoon, and a quickie divorce, you never know."

8. Happy/Unhappy

Happy/unhappy, they are saying how happy or unhappy they are. The Falcon says he is always happy, except when he's not, when the world breaks his heart with so much cruelty and no compassion, but what is happy or unhappy, anyway? He longs to cozy up to Simone. Now, that will likely make him happy. She says not necessarily, if he knows her track record and history with relationships. Instead, they eat Italian buns stuffed with salami, prosciutto and cheese, while the crazed, happy-to-be-unhappy driver grips the wheel, white-knuckled, determined to make Kingston in record time. To Simone's way of thinking, Elena is determined to storm and rage, wallow in unhappiness, until she has a chance to stick it to the barber. Elena pushes the Fiat 500 Pop, pedal to the metal, sucked along in the drag of semis, and shoots past cars twice or three times the Fiat Pop's size. She even races with SUVs.

Simone tells of the jealous men she has known, a parade of controlling lovers and woman-haters that force her to clear out at the first sign of abuse. She speaks about her parents' split, when as a kid, she lives in two places at once, and the bitterness between her mom and dad, and how many people are drawn into the contempt they have for each other, and the nannies that have taken care of her and raised her, while she bounces back and forth between an angry mother and an angrier father. They live up in the air and bounce off the walls. She makes a bid to stop bouncing and live on her own at sixteen when she can, always latching on to some guy or other until older men come sniffing around and take an interest with criminal intent and try to seduce her and own her, including the Shoemaker, sugar daddy to her sugar baby act.

"I was pregnant at sixteen," she says. "I thought of keeping the baby, but the father, a guy not much older than me, was a creep, phony, and worse, a pretend pimp. I couldn't stand him."

Elena asks her if she ever thinks about the kid. Sometimes, Simone says, and when the ache is bad, she regrets her decision, and makes herself suffer for it.

"Decision, the Falcon says. "It was decided the minute you were trapped, like being born a woman."

She turns to look at him, the Falcon, with his arms outstretched.

"Now, aren't you the sensitive guy?" she says, trying not to sneer.

"The Falcon is a feminist," Elena says, "right?"

"I love women," he says. "I feel their pain. I feel them when I get the chance. Unless you've cooked for a woman, you don't know them. I don't want to be one, just as I don't want a woman being me, but we can make each other happy or unhappy. My ma stood up to my pop for my sake, but got bopped. You see your mother getting thumped, and you're standing there as a kid, you want to kill him, but you freeze up. You spend the rest of your life getting back at him, but you don't know why she stays. Man, that makes you love women; love their secret power, their bodies and their way of sticking things out."

Simone is giving him the benefit of the doubt. Jive is jive. Is he being sincere? She is beginning to trust him, believing him. Elena isn't buying it. She has a pickle up her ass, as the Falcon says, and isn't enjoying it. She has seen his approach with other women. She has even dated him once or twice. He makes a mean bean salad and great pasta dishes. At least, with the Falcon, you'll get a good dinner and breakfast. Everything is a joke, except for food and humanity.

Awake again and doing her best not to bounce off the walls, as Simone has already said, happy/unhappy/happy/unhappy, the human rigmarole. Surprised by the joyless times in a relationship, everybody is trying to get away from everybody else. For her, a man who fills her with dreams and does what he wants with her body, and then leaves his mess and simply walks away, only to see somebody else. That is Duncan, and then just starting, the Lonely Barber.

"Everybody's distracted," the Falcon says. "Nobody can delay gratification. Everybody's afraid. Everybody's got a conspiracy theory to explain his or her feelings of terror. We're going to pass by the Nuclear Power Station, that makes two of them so far, and if it blows, we'll all be part of a glass-lined crater, and what will any of this matter? And sex, sex is under attack, with the switch-hitting, and free-for-all. I mean, I remember when teachers used to tie up our shoes, now their dodging bullets in the school hallways. The world has changed. And so can be cruel sometimes."

Simone is the only one listening. Is the Falcon crying, or falling asleep in the backseat, or both?

"Cruel world," the Falcon says. "The world is a cruel place. I know,

I know it can be kind. But when I hear that a bitch, a Cocker Spaniel mother dog, was found on a roadside."

"What are you talking about?" El asks. "You're raving."

"She had tears in her eyes," the Falcon says, "sitting next to a fish and chip carrier bag stuffed with her dead puppies."

"Shut up."

"Who would do that?" he demands. "The pups are dead, and she's lying there crying. It breaks my heart. Who would dump her next to the bodies of her dead pups, crying? I want to take care of that mother dog."

The Falcon cries himself to sleep. His head is thrown back, mouth wide open, he is snoring, he is blissfully dreaming. He's been asleep since uttering the word "mother." In his dream, he rescues the bitch and her pups. Another crying jag gets erased.

When Simone looks out the window, it is getting darker across the fields. What is she doing with these two? She has her reasons: something to do with getting away from the city for a while; maybe, something to do with catching up with the man she knows as Lonely to explain herself. Could it be she is falling for the Falcon? Simone sees her own face as in a darkened window, and then she stops looking.

9. THE THOUSAND ISLANDS

Jude and Marta stop at Cobourg and go to the beach and have an ice cream cone. Then back on the road, but they overshoot Kingston and head for Gananoque on the St. Lawrence, instead. They have lunch at the Inn and set out on a boat cruise of The Thousand Islands. It feels like a stolen honeymoon, just as Marta has said. Jude tells her he has been here before with a "friend," but it never worked out between them.

"I was in university then," he says, "when I thought I was going to be an actor, or a writer, an artist, maybe a teacher. I was accepted twice to the Art School, but each time, something got in the way, illness, or another opportunity."

"So you're not only a barber," Marta says, realizing the range of his interests and talents.

He tells her he wants something different, and simple.

"The way things were for my grandfather's generation," he says.

Still, what is he getting away from? Simple is hard when the world has changed, and keeps changing. Is it better or worse?

He tells her he has worked hard since childhood. He likes working. He has worked in the local library, ushered at the movies, has become a young manager, wearing a shirt and tie, and worked through school. He has tried acting with some success. That is how the barbering comes about. One of the older actors tells him backstage that he needs a trade to help him make a living when the theatres are dark. He can also get himself a tux and be a waiter. He has done that, too, for a while. He has even written about it, and the wildness of private parties. Yes, he writes on the side, poems, plays, stories, a novel. Some of his stuff has been published. He will show it to her sometime later. But it can't pay the bills. You have to make a living. He has taught school, worked as a college professor. He has to decide to go back to school for further qualifications, or strike out in a new direction. He has debts, but who doesn't? Everybody he knows, including the people he works for. The dialogue he has had with d'Arborio is nothing in comparison to the hostile blatherskite he has had to face with City Hall bureaucrats in getting a shop going.

"It used to be so easy, wasn't it? How is it that people with little or no education buy property and set up grocery stores, beauty salons, shoemaker shops, laundries, restaurants, and convenience stores? My grandfather on my dad's side was a shoemaker, but refused to take up the trade once he landed in Halifax. He spent his working days up on a roof, a roofer rather than go back to his trade. He did it without speaking a word of English in the early years. Bought a house. Paid off his mortgage. Raised a big family. When he died, he wasn't in debt."

Jude wishes to be like his grandfather, the real deal, to work and live in an honest and direct way; the way it is in his grandparents' time. No commuting, doing his best to endure gridlock, road rage, the weather, the losing game of living beyond your means, spending and getting with no power and no influence, and taxes, taxes, taxes. Just work, that's what he wants, real labour.

"A man must toil," his grandfather says. "Is it any work for a man, even flipping burgers? If it is, do it."

That type of talk means little or nothing anymore, but it means everything to Jude. He wishes to live in a real city. Cities can be real or unreal. He knows there are amazing places to live. Once on a trip out east, he falls in love with the Maritimes, P.E.I., in particular. Jobs or no jobs, for him, it is God's country. Still, the T.dot is real. It can be cruel and it can also be kind. He has lived in bed-sitting rooms, apartments, flats, and basements in different parts of the city: north on Dufferin, in the Annex, Korea Town, Liberty Village, north of Casa Loma in Forest Hill, and Little Italy. He has worked and studied in the city. He has written poems, plays, stories, and the city has been both his real and imagined landscape. All his fiction is about the city. The city has been kind to him. But making a living is a different story. He is looking for the heart of the city, and for what he can do to belong there. He wants an empathetic city, a city of compassion, city of mercy, city of toil. He wants the work of his hands to matter.

Then why is he seeking this mercy elsewhere? Can he leave behind what he has tried to do? Is he in a hurry to leave or scurry back when other places fail? No longer afraid to say how he has seen and experienced city life, he tells Marta that it is a benevolent, inarticulate giant that rescues and takes care of you, an underground of rivers and dark dreams that help you to come too close to the true heart of the city, or a film set where you can make a movie, shooting under a gibbous moon, east end escape routes, west end subway rides to find your theme, a city of raccoons and rats living with rich and poor, a human zoo.[16]

Marta says, "I hear where you're coming from."

It is a search for the "village" within the city. Toronto is nothing if not its neighbourhoods and towns and villages within the G.T.A. Talking this way, they settle in for the tour. Marta loves the water, the sights, and the islands. They kiss, like any honeymooning couple. Her lips are sweeter than any lick of an ice cream cone.

---

16   Cf. Nic Labriola's short stories

10. CALLING HOGS

So it is that the crowd in the Fiat 500 Pop hits the attractions in Kingston at the mouth of the Cataraqui and St. Lawrence rivers, Limestone City, for its grand 19th-century buildings, including the lakeside Kingston City Hall. The grand house and gardens of the Bellevue House National Historic Site commemorate Canada's first prime minister, Sir John A. Macdonald. Fort Henry, built in the 1800s, holds military demonstrations. Simone is reading the description on her Smart Phone. They eat at Chez Piggy. That has them laughing throughout the meal. Everything they see, do and speak about comes back to the pig.

"Man, pigs can park here for a buck, a loony, for the whole hog, the whole day."

"Can't do that in T.O.," Simone says.

"What's the plan now? Be serious, oink, oink," he snorts. "What are we planning to do if and only if we catch up to him, providing he's even here? Did he leave Hog Town only to live with the pigs? And what is that randy pig doing here, anyway? Are we out to slaughter him?"

"My guess is he's checking out the barbershops," says Simone. "Pretty driven. Picturing if he can set up here."

"Let's leave this trough and head down to the pig pens downtown," the Falcon says.

"Stop it, asshole," Elena says. "Enough is enough."

"In a pig's eye," he says, "I will. Soo-ee."

"What are you doing?"

"Calling hogs. Pig Calling. We're from Hog Town calling all hogs."

"You butchered enough of them," Elena says.

"Sausages, chops, pickled pig's feet," he says. "Now, what's the plan?"

"Catch up to him," Elena says. "Catch him."

"Switch cars."

"Force him in with El," Simone suggests.

"They can fight it out from there."

"What do we do with the chick he's with?"

"I'm sure you can think of something," Elena says.

She wants them to split up, walk around, and ask questions.

"Why not go to the cops, put in a missing person's?" asks the Falcon.

"No, no cops," she says. "Are you that stupid?"

"You calling me stupid, porky?"

"Let's go for a walk," Simone says, and, locking arms with the Falcon, leaves Chez Piggy.

"That piglet will pay this time," he says to the waitress on his way out. "Soo-ee."

They walk downtown. Simone pops a pill.

"You don't need that shit," the Falcon says. "Void the *Opioids*. Spoils the appetite and messes with you and your groove."

"Takes the edge off," she says. "This whole thing has got me rattled."

"You want to see him yourself, don't you?"

"Well, we never finished the date," she says. "I know he got hit pretty hard on my account. I'm feeling responsible."

"You still have a thing for him," the Falcon says, trying not to be disappointed.

"I guess," she says, and kisses him hard on the mouth. "But I'm with you now."

"Love the one you're with," he says. "Or show your pork more warmth."

Has her laughing, but she pops another pill.

"You're being kind to her," Simone says.

"Who? Elena? I feel bad for her. She's got it bad."

"Do you think she's not really pregnant?"

"Faking it?"

"An hysterical pregnancy, I don't know."

"She's so desperate."

"It's crazy."

"Let her play it out."

"She's like her grandfather. Has to have things her way. Stubborn, you'd think they're Calabrese."

As if in response to idle speculation, the Falcon gets a call from Elena.

"Where are you?" she asks.

"Close, just getting some alone time, you know, giving piggy-back rides, and making a pig of myself."

"Come back," she says. "Come back to the pig place."

"What's up? Did you find him?"

"I'm bleeding, covered in blood."

"A stuck pig."

"I'm going to hemorrhage, bleed to death."

Miscarriage? Elena is in the washroom where they find her. Rush her to Hotel Dieu, the Urgent Care. They stare at her in Emergency, as if it is a botched abortion.

"Do you want to keep it?"

"What do you think? Yes."

"Look, we're just trying to figure out what's happening."

It is then that Simone calls Jude on his cell.

"You need to get down here," she says.

"Where? What do you want? You took off on me," he says. "I took a hell of beating for you."

She tells him they are in Kingston looking for him.

"What for?"

"We've been following you, asshole."

"Who?"

She says *who*, and then says, "She needs you."

"What are you talking about?"

"She's pregnant. You're the father."

"The hell I am."

"You knocked her up."

"Who says?"

"She says she's bleeding, and may lose it."

Simone tells Jude again where they are.

"I'm not in Kingston," he tells her.

"You're somewhere near," she says.

"Near," he says. "Gananoque."

Their story may have ended, or a new chapter may have begun, but he agrees to travel to Kingston. Jude and Marta get to the hospital as quick as they can. He is suddenly left alone with Elena. What she has wanted all along, she finally has up to a point. She won't say whether she has lost the baby or not, no info about how far along she is, all pain and more drama. Jude feels bad. He feels sick. What the hell has he done? Can he believe her? Believe her or not, he has to man up.

The plan is to get back to Toronto soon. Jude will drive the Fiat 500 Pop and Marta will drive the Karmann Ghia. Too crowded for three, impossible for three, but the Falcon says it will be cosy.

"Cosi fan tutti," he says.

"Sorry, Marta," Jude apologizes.

"I guess, the honeymoon is over," she says, slipping into the Karmann Ghia with the Falcon and Simone.

"Yeah, when your ex has a bun in the oven, another happy mommy," says the Falcon. "The tummy is a game-changer."

He braces himself for smacks from all directions and isn't disappointed. Elena hits him the hardest. She knows how and takes advantage of her expertise. They climb into their designated cars, like racing car drivers.

"Next stop, Little Italy," the Falcon says, "safest place for a guy like me (and for my hair) to be."

Now in a sudden U-turn, the Karmann Ghia follows and chases after the canary-yellow Fiat 500 Pop. Two cars play cat and mouse on the 401, Highway of Heroes, heading westbound into the setting sun. Has anyone seen a black Hummer in the rear view mirror?

PART THREE

1. THE QUEEN BEE, *REPRISE*

river's side window rolled down, a bee flies in. Jude starts
swatting like a son-of-a-bitch, as he says later.

"It's the Queen Bee," he says. "Man, she's been following
me since Toronto."

"I had to follow you, track you down, bring you back," Elena says,
"before my family finds out. They'd treat you worse than my grandfather
did. He'll treat you worse just to prove he can."

"El, you're not shitting me," he says. "You lying?"

"No shit," she says, "no lies. You can take a paternity test, if you
think I'm trying to trap you."

"Everything's falling apart," he says. "No shop, and now this."

"I didn't lose the baby," she shouts, "just have to rest. Complete bed
rest, they said at the hospital."

"I'll get you back to the city as fast as I can," Jude says.

"What are you going to do?"

"Don't know."

"You couldn't stay put," she says. "That's your problem. I gave myself
to you, and you dumped me twice, three times."

"I was busy," he says. "I was in the middle of a deal. I was working
on the shop."

The barbershop in the romance of city life, should he hate it, the
idea of it, and what it has cost him?

"You can't dodge every bullet."

"A bullet and/or a paternity suit."

The trip will be too long with accusations and recriminations, if
they go on like this. He doesn't hate her. She doesn't hate him anymore.
He is lost. She has found him, but he doesn't want to be found. The
bee is still buzzing in the car. They duck their heads and swat their
arms, but at least they aren't eating ice cream cones at the time. The bee
buzzes against the windshield, finds a new flight path, and flies out the
open window. It goes away laden with the honey, as Jude thinks about

it, of his summer's day, and his spoiled honeymoon.

2. ROAD SONGS

No police or prosecution, once they get back, nobody is pressing charges. They each have something to hide and each has something on the other. Living in the same neighbourhood, they know the rules and know what is what.

Behind them, and sometimes pulling up along side them, overtaking them, and then drifting back, the crowd in the Karmann Ghia rocks to the tunes on the radio.

"What's your favourite song?" the Falcon asks Marta.

"'Bridge Over Troubled Waters,'" she says, smiling.

The Falcon belts out the song until he can't reach the high notes.

"What about you, Simone?"

"'Born to be Wild.'"

"Right on," he says. "Get your motor running, and your motor can really run."

He gets them to sing along.

"And you?"

"Always had a thing for Gianni Morandi, especially, "In Ginnochio da Te," "Non Son Degno di Te." And on this side of the Atlantic, I connect with old tunes, you know, like "The Wanderer," and "Runaround Sue," and I have my deep-dark reasons and other secrets, and if you're good, maybe one day, I'll let you in on them."

He launches in with gestures and does his best to defend his choice against allegations of sexism, and looks over at Simone and then looks around at Marta.

"But there's nothing like hip-hop and rap," the Falcon says to his captive audience.

The concert begins balls out, as he says, with Tupac, Dr. Dre, Eminem, Jay Z, even Drake. The Falcon sings one of his own tunes, which has them clapping and coming in on the chorus that makes them laugh.

In the Fiat 500 Pop, Elena asks Jude what he thinks he's doing leaving the city. Is he getting away from her? He says not everything is about her. The news has something to do with it, right? Now, don't cry. Keep your mouth shut, or you're likely to suck back another Queen

Bee, and it'll get stuck down your throat. What the hell are they ever going to do? She knows what her grandfather wants her to do, if he finds out. Jude says his, too, if he ever finds out, getting El pregnant, and then introducing him to Marta, another girl, messing around. Be a man. Be a real man. Man up. But that is what has landed him here with Elena. The shop will have to be taken apart, taken down, dismantled, *The Lonely Barber*, Lonely No More, and no more a shop. She says he can be Lonely somewhere else. Leave Little Italy? The point is the Retro thing. It has something to do with being half-Italian. Which half? Never mind that. Toronto is a place with its districts, villages, zones, and towns all within the GTA. Find a garage down a lane and build a shop. Why Elena's grandfather has connections, doesn't he? He can, if Jude wants, help him find what he is looking for. But he does not want it that way. His way or no way is how Jude puts it.

"You need help," she says. "I'll help you, that's all I ever wanted to do."

They will figure out about the baby thing later once they hear its first cry. The Fiat 500 Pop zips past Bowmanville, Oshawa, Whitby, Ajax, Pickering, and Scarborough.

Then the gravitational force of the Don Valley pulls the car south, two cars with the Karmann Ghia coming a close second, to the Bloor cut-off south, then under the viaduct. Man, the Luminous Veil looks beautiful, considering the streetlights and a huge moon. Rosedale Valley down to Gerrard, and through Cabbage Town, then on to Carleton and College Street, and they are home.

By Midnight, they are sitting in the Café Del Pop: Jude, Elena, Marta, Simone and the Falcon. He goes to the kitchen to whip up a midnight meal.

"Not a snack, but a whole feast," he says, "for the homecoming."

Since he has found out Lonely's real name, he keeps saying:

"St. Jude, patron saint of hopeless cases. We are hopeless, but beautiful. God help us."

Everybody is serving everybody else with the manager saying he has his staff back just in time to fire the whole effing bunch, and if he does that will *learn* them to bugger off and leave him short-staffed. But tonight, it is a reunion. So, live and let live. *Let the dead deal with the dead*, but let the living eat.

3. Moving the Shop

The coffee and desert over with, it is decided that everybody will be helping to gut and move *The Lonely Barber*, the unopened barbershop. Who will bring what, the tools, the cardboard boxes, the van and sandwiches (the Falcon), and who will take stuff to store for a while until the new shop is ready (Marta), and who will patch and paint the walls to get them back to their original colour, puke, (Simone volunteers)? It is also decided that Elena has to rest. She has lost blood, and it is too risky for her to get involved, but she can start making calls, and check things out on the Internet. She also has to break the news to her family. Pregnancy and family expectations are seldom, if ever, easy to bring together in these circumstances. The Shoemaker will likely want to take control of the situation. Jude can't believe the outpouring.

"This is your shot," says the Falcon. "At the risk of being crude, don't be rude, Jude (aka. Lonely). Don't vomit on your sweater, already. Don't puke up mom's spaghetti, as Enimem says. This is your shot. Take it. We're all here for you."

All this is getting too personal for Jude, and he says so.

"The personal is political," the Falcon says. "This is my brand of personal politics, getting things done for the human family, my brothers and sisters."

The Falcon grabs hold of Jude and gets him in the clinch. He only lets him go when Jude says that he is *touched*.

"Say you're touched."

"I'm touched," Jude says, trying to wriggle out of the bro embrace. "I'm fucking touched, and so are you, but in the head."

"Hey, watch the hair."

"One day, I'm going to cut it off, and make a new man out of you."

"No hair," the Falcon insists, "and no identity. You can't *falcon* around with the Falcon and you can't pluck his sleek, black feathers, his plumage, so to say, without destroying the high-flying bird."

4. Elena & the Shoemaker

When Elena goes in to her grandfather, he is sitting up in bed, plumping his fat pillows even fatter. She wants to help him, and maybe, make the bed, air out the room. The old man looks rundown, broken, beaten, defeated, but says no thanks to her. He insists that he is on the mend. She tells him straight out what has happened, not wanting an interrogation, lecture, sermon, a bawling out, a verbal beating or a rant. He interrogates her, lectures, sermonizes, bawls her out, verbally beats her, and rants, despite her straightforward account. She is determined not to cry in front of him. She doesn't want to give him the satisfaction, to hell with the old man. The gist of his ravings is that he has been beaten at his own game, beaten by a coward, a bullshit artist, a screw-up, and a born loser. He has lost the game (and now his grandchild) to a barber. No, not a barber, it's different for a real barber, but a wannabe, an upstart, a guy who knows nothing about the business and the business of business, defeated by old laws. He needs to be beaten, put in his place once and for all, make him bleed, make him crawl, make a man out of him. Conclude the business.

She reminds him that he has already given Lonely quite a good shit kicking, jumped him, remember, and kicked his ass. What good does it ever do? He says she is right up to a point. Some guys have heads liked sucked eggs, and all they understand is pain, but some guys are egomaniacs and pain means nothing to them. They gain nothing but a sense of heroism. They think they're urban saints, crusaders, ready to die for some hopeless cause.

No matter what he is, she says, he is the father of her baby. Unborn, he says. And yes, she is sure it is his. Has done the test, drugstore bought, and seen a doctor, the signs are there, not to mention what has happened in Kingston. She wants to keep it. She needs rest, or risks losing the baby. Is that what he wants?

The Shoemaker twists it, turns and tortures the situation. He wants to fix it, bend it, and mend it with invisible patches. He goes on and on about what he has done for her over the years, right from the beginning. How Elena's father is no good, a real shit. What good is he? And the way he takes off to Italy for escape holidays? And what is he doing now, besides screwing around along the Adriatic coast, doing nothing? Elena sleeps around with every nonentity—what does she expect? Half of them she picks up at the Café. But she denies it, and says Lonely is different. He gets you all excited about things, life, and plans. With his kind of talk, he is so open to anything and anybody, and this *openness* is . . . never mind. He never defers his dreams.

"An empty elevator shaft," her grandfather says, throwing off the bed sheet, sitting up in his underwear on the edge of the bed. "An elevator shaft," he interrupts her with malice. "Doors open. You step in. No floor. You fall to your death in an elevator shaft. Ask where is he, if he survives? Dreaming somewhere, scheming, freefalling until he lies at the bottom of the shaft."

Elena tries a couple of angles in Lonely's defense. She also gets her grandfather his silk robe and drapes it over his regal shoulders and the rest of his naked body. What does her defense of the barber really amount to? If she opens her mouth, her grandfather says, a King again, he will close it for her with a backhand. And yes, hitting a pregnant woman doesn't bother him. What does he want her to do?

"Stop fooling around, and stop getting involved with these losers."

He will take care of it, as always.

"Get some rest. Sleep. Don't give it another thought."

He says he will fix it.

"Anything broken can be mended again. No tears. Relax. Relax. You're my fucking granddaughter, right? And you don't know how lucky you are, I'm your grandfather."

He wipes away Elena's tears. She's crying for herself, but hates doing it.

"There, there."

He blows her nose with the silk handkerchief from the pocket of his robe. Her grandfather will take care of it. That is what he will do. Mending is his specialty, and stock and trade. But that is what she is most afraid of.

He sends her away, gets dressed, and tries to figure things out. So, the victim has beaten him at his own revenge game twice. Still, it can be managed. The Shoemaker spends the rest of the day making his rounds of the neighbourhood. He orders a new blue suit from the tailor, and what the hell, he also has his Shadows sized for new suits. They just got back from their reconnaissance work out east. They don't deserve the new suits, but the Shoemaker wants them to match and not clash with his style and fashion sense. There's going to be a wedding, and he's got the shotguns, if necessary, to shoot at the church bells.

"You see this bespoke suit," he says to them. "It drives the ladies wild and it intimidates the men. That's what it's for. It has something to do with the cut and the embroidery on the back and the right sleeve. Too many women have stopped me in the street to say how much they love this jacket. Love the jacket. Love the man."

They will look like a *doo-wop* group from the nineteen-fifties. He loves singing the old tunes, anyway. He then stops by to see his sister, Graziella, a nurse working at the drug store, doing piercings that day. He reminds her that when he wants her opinion regarding family matters, he'll ask for it, or speak to his own ass for an intelligent piece of advice, the implication being that his asshole is smarter than her mouth, and that she has an asshole for a brain. Otherwise, he says for her to keep her mouth shut. He has been hearing things lately, and she is the source of the leaks. Graziella swings and strikes back (she won't be intimidated or infantilized) by saying that, although their mother and father have claimed they are flesh and blood (brother and sister), her heart and his heart are as far apart as Heaven from Hell.

That is how they talk to each other. She tries to tell him that she is in her early sixties now and not a kid anymore and that he can't speak to her that way, and that she'll speak up if and when she feels like it on any topic, including the rumours and allegations of his dealings in the neighbourhood, shaming the family as he is. She has an audiotape of their mother's deathbed confession and swears she will use it against him when the time comes. She also tries to tell him to roast in hell, but she knows he will never die. He has condemned himself to everlasting hell on earth. The devil is gong to shit on his grave. He doesn't care if she speaks or not as long as she keeps her mouth shut or else. Or else what? Not even the dogs will know where to find her, he says, and only he and possibly his ape-necked Shadows know what he means by that. He refuses an ear piercing, threatens her with a lethal piercing of his own, if she does not heed his warning, and leaves the drugstore. But he doesn't leave in a fit or state of indignation, anger or resentment. Instead, he forgets about it at once. And, as soon as his shiny shoes hit the sidewalk, he erases his sister, Graziella, from his memory. She is as far away from his thoughts as salvation is from damnation.

Once outside, he gives money to a homeless woman dressed in a long, leather coat, and smoking a cigarette, as she pushes her shopping cart piled up with her worldly possessions. He doesn't like giving charity to the homeless, but she looks like a favourite aunt of his, now dead, and resembles his mother. One of the Shadows suggests to the other one that maybe it is his mother, who knows? But you can't mention his mother and live.

Then he stops in for an espresso at the Bar Italia and sings an aria from Puccini, *Nessun Dorma*, one of his best renditions, and orders cognac for himself, nothing for his "shady companions." They leave the bar. It's growing dark. It's growing blue. As he walks along College Street, he talks about family secrets. Open secrets of the family, he calls them. The Shoemaker insists that they exist in every family.

Nobody talks about them. They are too dark. In the Shoemaker's family, the dark secret is that everything has been decided long ago, long before events actually happen. By that, he means it is prearranged, preordained, if you like, and he does like, so he can say straight out that it has to do with money, if there is any, and power, and there are always positions of power in every family, even (and especially if) there is no fucking money, as the Shoemaker likes to say. But in his family, there is money, money made on the backs of his father who toils day and night to make it and save it, at the expense of his health, and his mother's health and sanity; and his mother who when her husband dies takes it on herself to save the family fortune for the rest of them, her desire being to leave them something, anything, even a hat pin, as she puts it. But the point is who will manage this money, this untold wealth? Still, they never know how much it is, or at least the others don't because the Shoemaker is the chosen one; he is chosen to keep the money safe, all right, make sure his mother has enough all her days, and keep the open secret that he is the banker, you know, the gray eminence, the silent figure. So, he doesn't have to speak, and he is perfectly willing to tell the others to take off or shut their mouths, because, though they think they love their mother, the point is she has chosen him to manage the funds. Life is cruel; it kills you off. Some of the bereaved are relieved; others are inconsolable. For him, the only solace is money. The problem is that although he has money, he is good with it, but others aren't; and although he has signing power, feeling that he has power over life and death matters, he doesn't like people, and doesn't really give a shit what happens to others, so long as they do what he says, and that applies now to his granddaughter, Elena, and to the Lonely Barber. What the fuck is his real name anyway? He'll be family soon, whether he likes it or not. It applies to his granddaughter and the guy she hooks up with and the baby when it is born.

"Especially the little bugger," he says. "But blood is fucking blood, and family is fucking family. It's my business if I don't like any of them. But nobody is going to fuck around with my goddamn family."

5. Jude & Marta

Jude isn't really trying to justify himself, but that's how it comes out. He has had a good time with Marta, he admits, what with the trip to his hometown and then the boat cruise to the 1,000 Islands, a honeymoon, that is how it feels, and that is what it is, sort of. But he has been on other stolen honeymoons, and, one in particular, has caught him with a baby bump.

Marta says she is cool with it. She is cool with everything. And down with it. The way things turn out, or how things don't ever turn around, never matter much to her. She is in it for the fun of it, the way one thing rolls into another, one day into another day, one moment into another moment. She is an improviser. The dialogue has to set up the partner; otherwise the improvisation dies.

She says it is scar tissue. Her body is a wound, but healed over from past disasters. No commitments mean survival, endurance, self-protection for years of self-neglect. No obligations and *s'all good*, all things being equal. No strings, no claims, no chains, nothing that binds, or blinds. She knows what time it is. Nothing hurts that way. Not much, anymore. She is open to everything, chaos, too. No sure thing. The moon is waning, a Waning Gibbous Moon, in its phase, and they are saying the universe is dying, they have proof, so why sweat the small stuff, the missed opportunities, the right guy, but at the wrong time? Does he have to answer for the past, or even last night?

Sorry. Still he keeps saying sorry. Jude is sorry the way things are, and the sorry drift and tide of events. He admits that taking her to meet the grandparents is too much, too soon. Not sleeping together, not having sex anymore? That is the way it is, and how it is. But taking Marta to see the grandparents in the hometown, that is a form of seduction as with a puppy dog inside your jacket peeking out, but just enough to make it hurt. Unless? Unless the wound is a cut into scar tissue, and you never feel the wound, only the jest.

"No hard feelings," she says.

She has a friend in the East end, owns a salon, that maybe will give her some advice, a lead or two, she will call her. Leslieville is nice, a great part of the city. It will be ideal for a shop.

Jude says there already are barbershops in Leslieville doing great business. He has worked there for a while, honing his skills. But it is certainly worth taking another look, especially with her.

"Why especially with me?" Marta asks, not really wanting an answer.

"Because maybe, the honeymoon is not over yet," Jude says.

"Nothing is over until it's over," she says. "Even then, sometimes it never ends."

6. THE FALCON & SIMONE

"You look tasty," the Falcon says. "I could eat you up with a spoon."

"I'm nobody's *edible woman*," Simone says.

"*Edible* means *eatable*," the Falcon says. "Is it a cookbook? I'd like to get a recipe or two to add to my book."

"It's a novel," Simone says. "I've read the book, and met the author at a signing, not for that one, *The Edible Woman*, but for *Stone Mattress*."

"That'd definitely do a number on your back," he says. "Who *dat*, doing the nasty on a mattress made of stone?"

"Margaret Atwood."

"Whoa, rock on," he says. "But don't *Margaret-Atwood* me. No disrespect intended, but the word around the neighbourhood is that she's broken many a man's back with her books. Felt the chill on my spine, when you mentioned her name, the spine-tingling authoress."

"*Author*," Simone says. "And we're not doing that anymore."

"What? What are we not doing anymore? By the way, what are we doing now?"

"The sexist thing, the male trick, the gender thing, we're not doing it anymore."

"Right, right, the gender, transgender, trannies with new transmissions, revved up. Get in. Get it on. Let's go."

He opens the passenger side door, and Simone climbs into the Fleetwood Caddy. She has brushed up against him because he wants her to, and because she still wants to get a rise out of him, confusing the gender thing. The Falcon slides off the hood and scoots round to the driver's side, hops in, starts the engine and speeds off.

"Trans-persons, gender-variant, two-spirit women, and women of non-binary sexual orientations," the Falcon says. "Should I?"

"What?"

"Read her. Margaret, you know."

"Are you really going there?"

"Why not? It's in the script between a man and a woman these days. Besides, you like her. I like you."

"She's funny, sexy."

"You're shocking me now, a ball-cutter and sexy?"

"She's not *that*," Simone says. "You should read her."

"On the wrong side of history," he says. "At least, on the wrong side of the city."

"I live here, and I read her," Simone says.

"True," he says, "too true. She's done you good. For me, I like reading people, places, you know. I like to read the city, like an open book. Through my eyes, reading the city's legible landscape: along the tagged walls of urban and suburban sprawl, links to the rural route roads, the past, re-imagined, the future, dreamed of, or the other way around, because the city as a body is a body and has a body, fretwork of urban slang from *lish* to *sugaring*. Virtue of riding along the roads, or when our parents knew the Boys of Major Lane, who together went off to war, 1940, and *how* neighbourhoods and *why* neighbourhoods and *when* neighbourhoods and *where*: our urban book. Get Atwood to write it, and I'll maybe read it. The Toronto Look."

"What do you read?"

"All right, I just read a book, graphic novel, no less."

"Graphic?"

"About this freaking bike thief: we've changed his city, so he has the right to steal our bikes."

"I remember reading about it: guy stole thousands of bikes, stored them in different shops."

"No joke, he's got theories."

"Conspiracy theories, no doubt."

"Who doesn't? But the book with pictures makes his case. He's crazy, maybe, but crazy like a fox. Got me thinking about T.O. The way it used to be, the way people wanted it back then, and the way it is now, the way we want it. Mel Lastman Square? Fordville? Tory Town? The mayor we elect, we seem to deserve, depending on how we cook up our city."

"Where you taking me?" Simone asks.

"West End. Check out a couple of barbershops. See what you think. Get Lonely set up, if we can help out."

"You're thinking of El."

"Sure. She's a good kid. Needs help, too. Not from her grandfather, but from friends like us. Maybe, who knows? Maybe, she and Lonely, you know, can figure it out and get the dark romance going again. They like it dark."

The Falcon suggests driving to Bloor West Village to check out Demone's, the Runnymede Barber Shop, and Mino's. A reconnaissance mission, as he says, to get the lay of the land.

"Maybe, they're hiring."

"I think he wants his own place."

"So maybe, they're retiring. Maybe, they're selling. The only problem is how do we visit three barbershops without letting anybody touch my hair?"

"Maybe, you're a sweet guy," she says. "But for sure, you're a smooth customer. I'm certain you'll figure it out."

"Just trying to help out," he says.

"Then you're definitely a sweet guy," Simone says.

"You won't ever know till you get a little lick, a little taste," he says. "A Taste of Little Italy: Me."

"*The Edible Man*," Simone says.

"Now, if I'm in that book, I'm reading it."

"Maybe, I'm writing it."

"Simone Atwood, I like it. Am I going to be in it?"

"We'll have to see, won't we?"

"Put me in your book, it'll be a bestseller," he says, almost singing it. "It'll all be true, if you're in it, too, or true lies. The hero is a lover, who knows how to cook, and his name is The Falcon, and his true love is a stunning falcon-trainer called Simone. That's the pitch, the blurb on the dust jacket."

"The Falconer," she says.

"The Falconer," he says, his voice soaring. "Let's fly to the West End."

7. Jude & the Shoemaker (with Duncan)

Jude agrees to meet the Shoemaker, provided they both come without muscle and no weapons, especially the straight razor. No shoe bombs either and no concealed knives, no hammers and nails and no scissors. The place they agree upon is the Café Dip, but only outside on the Patio, at the back away from College Street. Just coffee, no food, straight talk and no bullshit, agreed.

"I thought I'd never have to see you again."

"Same goes for me."

"No cards?"

"Forget it."

"Not even Scopa?"

"Well, you got me here. Now what?"

"I know what you've done."

"So does the whole street."

"I also know what you're going to do."

"That so? Because I don't know what I'm going to do, how is it that you know before I do?"

"You're going to do right."

"Look, if you think."

"I don't think. I act. My time, guys died for less than I'm talking."

"People kill for more than love these days, or get killed."

"Don't give me love, not what you did to her."

"My grandfather would likely think the same, do the same, or threaten to, or say the same. I think that'd he agree with you. 'Be a man,' he says."

"Your grandfather sounds like my kind of man. Maybe, I mistook you."

"You did already. I've been mistaken before."

"Huh, well, you beat me, no mistaking that, fair and square. You played and beat me at my own game."

"You beat me at mine. We're even, but for you know who."

They were thinking the same thing: Elena.

"Right, even, but for her."

"I can't marry her, Mr. d'Arborio. Too quick, if marriage is on your mind, if a shotgun wedding is in my immediate future, in the cards, in the offing, as they say."

"No offing, no knee-capping, no wedding plans yet. Is there even a baby? We'll soon find out. It could be hysteria, deceit, at this point we don't know, and we're taking her word for it. I want to believe her. But first things first: money."

"I don't have any."

"I do."

"Well, I'm not going to marry you, unless I have to."

"You don't know what you're missing, and I got a cane and credit cards. But I also have money and contacts."

That is when Jude sees Duncan. He waits on them, and serves the agreed-upon coffee. Jude stands up.

"Sit down. Have your coffee."

"I thought we agreed."

"We did. He's been dealt with. That's why he's no trouble for you, and why he's wearing shades and limping. No trouble anymore for me, but he comes bearing gifts—coffee and a contract."

"I'm not signing anything."

"You're refusing?"

"I'm not accepting."

"No contract to sign, just saying he's got an offer. So refuse it, but hear him out. He practiced what he's got to say. He stayed up all night long learning it."

Duncan sets down the coffees and begins talking. He has some teeth missing, so his speech is slurred.

"Shipping locker available for you; freight container. Bathurst and Dundas, any colour, turn it into a barbershop. No rent. It's prepaid."

"I paid," the Shoemaker says, slurping his coffee.

"The Community is offering these boxes, crates, what you will, to help stimulate the area, bring in people, celebrate the neighbourhood. Not uptown, not the old, traditional neighbourhoods, but for recent immigrants, influx of people, or the invisible Torontonians, new colours. Imagine Toronto in a new way. Market 707. Man, it's got cache. Leave Little Italy. Get on over to Scadding Court. The cargo container could be your way out of here. What do you say?"

"I heard about it," says Jude. "Read about it, even took a stroll for a look see when I was looking at options for the shop."

"Don't say anything until you've seen it at least. Dream inside the *box.*"

Then Duncan runs out of things to say. His mouth won't work. He pulls out a manila envelope.

"A little donation for the trouble we put you through, a wedding gift from what I hear. Congrats! I hope to dance with you on your wedding day."

"You can go," orders the Shoemaker, "or you'll be dancing on the tip of my shoe."

"Will there be anything else? Today's special for desserts?"

"Just the bill."

"I'll think about it," Jude says.

"The money is yours no matter what. It's an old debt now paid in full. You won, remember?"

"That's it?"

"Done. I'm old. I need another nap."

"I thought it was going to be a tougher negotiation."

"That's over with. I'm a changed old man, thanks to you."

"Losing changes a man, same as winning."

"Losing at cards, maybe. Losing love, always."

They both are thinking of the same person: *Simone.* At least, they have that loss in common. A sense of loss can bring people together. Empathy can build friendship. Friendship can lead to peace negotiations and a peace accord. Or it can conceal enmity, resentment, envy and spite. The victor and victim trade places. They know this much: that love can kill.

8. THE RETROFIT

Elena swears on her mother's grave (though she isn't dead yet) that she hasn't put her grandfather up to it. The Shoemaker needs no prompting from the likes of her to make proposals, offer, and get things arranged, managed and done. So she and Jude drive down to Dundas and Bathurst (Market 707 and the Scadding Court Community Centre) to check out these freight containers, retrofitted cargo containers, or lockers, *whatever.*

Jude actually gets excited when he sees the shops and feels the vibe. He can see the infinite possibilities (all right, the finite possibility) of setting up a barbershop here. It will be a different kind of romance. Isn't this how other trendy places get their start from Yorkville in the Sixties, Queen Street, part of Cabbage Town, Leslieville, the Beaches, Kensington Market, right? It has to start somewhere. Dope has something to do with it, Jude is saying. People want to smoke pot freely in the streets. The Toronto Look, they used to call it back in the day. The fledgling art scene or scenes in art and fashion, not to mention music, musicians, artists, writers, and a community comes up out of the smoke, attracts people, runaways, strays, artists, tourists, dealers, trades. Every era needs its own signature haircut: the duck's ass, crew cut, mop top, the mushroom, Mohawk, faux hawk, buzz, the fade. This place needs a barber. The organizers are thrilled to show the couple around the place with its cargo containers in all colours of the spectrum with metal doors. Pop them open and dream up a shop.

Jude can dream it. He starts pacing everything out for the chair, the coffee machine, and the mirror on the wall. He can cut hair, and shave his customers in a shipping container turned on its side. Music, coffee, and conversation, it is all about word-of-mouth.

"There's a great barber down there. Check him out, man. He's a writer and a barber. He used to be in Little Italy. Wild, yeah, wild, and fucking cheap."

He gets Elena excited with the picture he can paint within a cargo container and with the shop he can dream up in the city he can re-imagine. It will take off from Market 707.

But as they drive back to College Street, he isn't so sure. He can convince you of anything, and then convince you of the opposite. His misgivings turn to doubt. Can he support himself and a family, if that is the way things are going? Can he make a living, and earn a wage in a shipping container? He has to think about it.

"Think it over, and you'll see I'm right," Elena says. "You can do it. You can do anything you put your mind to."

He will think it over.

"It is doable," Jude says, "but just."

9. JUDE, ALONE

Jude finds himself alone, not lonely. He is outside the Crystal[17], the extension to the Royal Ontario Museum, called the Michael Lee-Chin Crystal, designed by Daniel Libeskind. Quick glance at steel and glass, he also hears kids' voices coalesce: cry for dinosaurs and raptor bones. Shopping bags and their carriers occupy the north shore, like a paved river, or chance the south-side flow of traffic. Metallic droning cabs and sirens seem never-ending. On the north shore, Jude sees an unsuccessful beggar that needs a talent beyond squalor to make ends meet. Needs to front a one-man band, but can't play a penny whistle, harp or fiddle the way some buskers can and do outside the Crystal's newly designed steel and glass.

He is carrying a cup of coffee he has bought at the Second Cup at Bloor and Avenue Road. A guy in a Subaru begins mocking him for walking with his coffee cup. The morning mocker wishes him a Happy Freaky Friday from his rolled down window, all the same, more of a threat than a fond greeting, especially from a stranger. Jude wishes he had one of his dad's jewelled shillelaghs, cudgels, canes, or Blackthorn walking sticks for cracking his skull.

He is thinking: "Don't get me wrong. I know the city can be cruel and can be kind, like any living act, one life form mocks another. But once I swaggered down these streets in revolution. Skyline passed by me in longhaired surrender. Got arrested at a protest in the late nineteen-nineties."

But gone is the morning mocker when he trips over to the curb to engage the smart-ass driver. Vanishing, he gets his wish, not Jude's: the coffee cup trembles in his fumbling fingers, then slips away from his self-mocking hand, and spills on the sidewalk. He has different views of the same city. For him, it is sometimes crazy town, or like Naples, see it and die, or see Toronto and live. What holds everything back for Jude (as the Falcon once remarked) *are slow misunderstandings, crawling along tagged walls, walking his bike (sometimes with a flat tire), even as*

17   The extension to the Royal Ontario Museum called the *Michael Lee-Chin Crystal,* designed by Daniel Libeskind.

the city holds him, away from the same moment together, always twice, two views of the same thing, dispute of time and place, disgrace of citizens, not living it, before he puts his name to it. Then the spin of the white nights (not satin as in the song by the Moody Blues), but the curated White Night, the curated city on Nuit Blanche, liquid crystal projects on alley walls, the street performances, competing with the daylight madness of artists preaching art. Two views of the night obliterate darkness. Night people stay up all night long so the homeless can finally get some merciful sleep, like Jude, dreaming up their new city.

He says to himself, "What's eating you, Clinton Avenue Romeo, as if your lover hangs from the second storey window on Clinton and College? You deserve the Balcony Scene, and what happens after the love story. Juiced-up lover, her grandfather thrusts you up against the wall when you walk her maidenhead home in the rain. He shoos you away like a bloated flesh fly from her wet lips. But on the other side of the street, away from any Juliet's house, in the magical realism of being young, you are on the threshold of the parkette, watching the park bench burn; the fire flashes along the grass to the trash bin. Sirens split the sound of a low-lying firestorm that crawls along the scorched ground, while you burn with regret and flick your cigarette."

At one time, he would have written these thoughts down in a Claire Fontaine Notebook with a black marker, but not now. Will he ever write poems and stories again?

Jude is thinking: "Comes a day when your sink is full of muck, not yours. Belongs to the upstairs' neighbour, as Marta said. What are you going to do about the mess in your sink? What kind of chaos are you talking, the kind that sees no evil, hears no evil, speaks no evil? Don't tell me you don't know, pleading innocence. You're to blame. What about pretending your shit doesn't stink? I'm here to tell you it does. Your shit stinks. That gold vehicle in the driveway is a gilded turd. Your golden-haired sex-machine protects you so nobody can find you. Your crap blocks the toilet and backs up the sink, *my* sink. It's your creation I'm talking about, neighbour. What are you going to do about your offering? Look into the pit. It's your shit. But I have to clean it up."

He can write something about it (Marta's story), but decides not to, so pre-occupied is he with the idea of his shop. Besides, he has written already about the spirit of the city: ways we have forgotten. What is it we are looking for and not what is in store for people like his father that September in 1969, and the story he tells of Varsity Stadium, as the band plays for Peace, but he gets away and hides in the room on Bedford Road, the place his dad calls the Pit. Is there any such thing as a city mystic, a citizen who doesn't reject anything, and accepts it all?

"Don't throw yourself away," his dad says. "Discard illusions."

But Jude howls, utters a wild cry of longing, and breathes desire's testament to follow up on his humanity, while a shop owner keeps shouting: "Just try it. Come on. Just try it."

Now, he is thinking about his sister, Donna. He feels bad for her. She is talented and uncertain, mixed up with a couple of guys. She has trouble deciding. Her indecision hurts her most of all. With regard to her, Jude thinks: "Don't agree to limits. Better to do nothing at all than hit the wall. Bound to it with every minute, a limitation. Every limitation leads to *inaction*. Better to do nothing, and that way, when day and night demand endless inactivity, negation and inertia make *nothing doing* exactly the same as *doing nothing*. Limitless ease of living for its own sake, living musically, attuned to the harmony of the spheres, tuned in to love that mocks all limits."

But what about his love affairs and spent love? Jude thinks it best not to think about the past. But it barges in, intrudes, and elbows its way into his thoughts. He thinks about an old girlfriend, now out of sight, but not out of mind. He doesn't like to think about her often. In the Trinity Library, she writes her last letter to him in dark blue to make it seem true; truer. Tries to tell you, but you won't listen; can't. Uncouple her chains from your crossed arms. Unlock the cellar door to her secret possessions. Objects float away from your flooded bedroom. Drowned in the burning bed, chained to the floor. Her letter reads: *Free your heart like an unfettered boat from the scoured basement's watery tomb. We failed together, but I won't be (or can't be) responsible for both our losses. Free yourself when you can, and so free me. Wrote this letter in blue for its tint and mood to make it true; truer.*

He finds himself walking up the Casa Loma Steps. Castle in the air did not crumble, but the dreamer did, and died. House that Henry built for the fairy tale love affair. His visions collapse. His millions vanish. City bureaucrats outwit the self-made man, one of the dead romantics. But on World Pride Day, 110 couples celebrate their love at a mass wedding, white gowns in twos flowing up and down the steps in *GrandPride*, spirit of the city in love. From the Casa Loma Steps, you can see the avenue that Henry dreams up only to ruin him. But still sleek joggers run up the breathless steps, and still Jude moves up one step at a time.

What is he looking for when he walks through the city? No more maps, or stars, just guesswork. Listen to the whistling sounds of night across uncharted streets. Into this silence, throw a word or two.

He is thinking: "Don't tell yourself everything you know about being here. Leave some room for discovery. Just a voice within, when you're gone. Breathe in the soundless air and strive with the key of this city to taste the story on your tongue. Passed by with nothing left to say, or so little that I couldn't hear it or remember it, passed by without a trace, and not away. But seasons flutter among tall pines. The way you sent me surprised me on the verge of becoming clear, questioning nothing, rejecting nothing, taking no offence beyond the passing season, its taunts and jests. At this late hour, I know what I was looking for, and then road signs, billboards, streetlights become the city."

Birds are fighting in the bushes. Jude thinks about his Aunt Catherine's pet bird. He has heard that the bird has died. His aunt calls it Birdy-Bird. Gone is the blue tail-feather sweep of its perch. Or, free flight, as it wings home through the wilds of the living room, announcing its own death with a bird in the house. Then squawks and talks a blue streak, preferring Wolfie's pa-pa-pa Papageno & Papagena's Duet to Ludvig Van's pa-pa-pa-pam. Or, on the shoulder, Birdy-Bird tells you: *It's Study time, study time.* Or, liking your hairdo, it pecks at it. And, on any given Sunday, whistles when you walk in, asking: *Is that you? Who's there?* But your bird is not. "What shall be missed, yet not surrendered to," thinks Jude, "is the way Birdy-Bird frames a blue-tinged question, or how he parrots you in love's surrender."

He is returning home, cycling his way across Toronto twilight on his Bianchi, and every new pathway is a bike path back home, riding home on his side of the road, to return to his place down the basement steps, not Marta's place. In wet moonlight, he is charting each bit of roadway it takes to move: to go where lamplight restores lost sight, no longer missing the neighbourhoods he has left behind. Or those that leave him for other towns and villages, other locations. One of his high school friends, Jay, is heading up north to Bobcageon's northern lights, and others in long V-formations fly south, and his brother is going west for the sake of the lake and rest of the ancient trees, and another is travelling east for the breeze whipping off the Atlantic, they veered off the same road, but he stays where he is staying for the time being. Reeling of the new direction tips the balance: city benediction, not elegies, or ruins. Yet a dark question rises up out of the core. Question: Do you miss the old city? What are you doing here now? Answer, as he answers it: "I'm thinking it over, and making plans. But I am really here for cutting hair."

10. The Distillery District Hook-Up

Marta is in the Distillery District, listening to the blues and jazz at the festival. She thinks she'll ring Jude up and give him a tip. She gets him on the cell.

"There's a little place down here for rent," she says. "Might be what you're looking for."

Jude takes the streetcar to the East end of the city. The Distillery District is all decorated for a Blues and Jazz Festival. This is summer in Toronto. Maybe, he'll be crazy lucky there. With music, music, music everywhere, he hooks up with Marta. She looks stunning, strikingly beautiful in her short skirt, sheer, white top, with hair swept back, shades, sun hat and sneakers.

She keeps thinking of him, she says, listening to the music and looking at the buildings of the old Gooderham and Worts Distillery. She keeps talking about the area. How great it would be to have his shop there. He doesn't say much, but listens. Is this the complicated kindness that they are talking about these days? He shouldn't be doing this. Is he in love with her? Is it real, or just a reaction to the pressure, the need for a woman who is serenely detached, complicated yet uncomplicated, intelligent, and kind? She shows him the sites, the shops and restaurants, the theatre.

Jude becomes jealous of her, missing her, thinking she will be with someone else, and not him. He is jealous, not of her past, but of her future, a future minus him. The more he subtracts himself, the angrier he gets. He kisses her. She responds.

They go from makeshift stage to makeshift stage, taking in the jazz and blues. Marta dances, and leans against him, and he holds her close. The buildings bulk up in front of them, around them, in a tight embrace. People have industrialized the city, built factory after factory, but now the Distillery is re-imagined as a space for restaurants, shops, Soulpepper Theatre, and music in the open air. Deindustrialization, right? With pedestrianization, the city can be reconfigured, fictionalized, to live in and live on.

What he wants is simplicity itself. Yet the simple things are no longer easy. They are spectral, illusive. The dream job is an apparition. People used to be able to come here with nothing and build a business, grow a family, ply a trade. He wants to work with his hands, standing on his feet all day, speaking to clients, giving them what they want, a good haircut, a good conversation, maybe, a beer. It is an endlessly revealing job. You can extend yourself through people forever.

Now, Jude knows the complicated sadness of a dream deferred. But Marta says the Distillery District is perfect for him: the tourists, even at Christmas, are an endless parade here, spiced up with Soulpepper Theatre, which keeps them coming. But what are the bylaws, the City Hall tangle and red-tape wrangle? What are the rents? You can hardly think of owning a place down in the Distillery, Jude thinks. But he lets her talk about it, dreaming in twos, isn't that love or its beginning? But that dream dies, doesn't it? Or do dreamers in love die harder?

They keep moving from building to building as the bands play the Blues. All Jude can do is to listen to the music and stare at Marta. What if people like her don't really exist?

PART FOUR

1. WANDERING IN THE ANNEX & THE NORTH END

Following a tip from a friend from beauty school, Bao, that he meets getting off the streetcar, Jude shoots down to the Annex. A new shop has opened up to challenge Gus the Barber and Makeover Barbershop and Spa. They are hiring at *Hairy's Place*. Jude isn't sure about the image: too ironic, too trendy. He peers inside: young, hip, great barber chairs. Is it what he wants? He walks in, chats up the managers. They are open to letting him prove himself and show them what he can do.

"Bring in your model," they say.

He says he'll be back in a bit. He thinks of calling the Falcon, but he knows Falconeri won't let him touch his hair. So he walks along Bloor and checks out the zone.

Guy is selling books at the corner of Brunswick and Bloor. Panhandlers with paper coffee cups call out for change. A woman on a blue milk crate in front of the bank chants: "Pregnant and hungry, anything will do." He thinks of Elena, pregnant, but not hungry, nor likely to be ever, safe in her own neighbourhood. At least, she won't have to sit on a milk crate begging. An old lady in a wheelchair, without any legs, and missing fingers and parts of fingers, keeps up her prayer: "Spare change, spare change." A blind guy is walking fast with his white cane, saying over and over: "Do you have a nickel or a dime or a quarter or a dollar? Do you have a nickel or a dime or a quarter or a dollar?" An old man in a long winter coat, despite the season and the heat, with long white hair, bearded, walks slowly by. Maybe, Jude can ask him to be his model. When he does, the wanderer looks terrified and shakes his head from side to side.

"A coffee? A muffin? A haircut? I could clean you up. You'd be a new man, or the man you were or thought you wanted to be."

The old man keeps walking away. He isn't begging, or asking for anything, just the right to drift, and the right to his own madness. His red-rimmed eyes implore Jude to leave him alone. Let him be. Jude wants to give him the best haircut of his life. It is the homeless guy in Oshawa all over again. This is what he wants to do—cut hair for free, groom the homeless, spruce up the street people.

He asks the bookseller if he will agree to get his haircut. He will, but he can't leave his books. It is his business, his livelihood. Business is brisk in the summer. Then Jude sees a homeless man in a black, shiny bubble coat begging in a doorway. He asks him, and the man says he will let him do anything he wants for a few bucks, as long as he doesn't have to take off his coat. The guy is short, always smiling. Jude takes him to *Hairy's Place*. The girl at the cash has seen the bubble coat before. She wonders if it is Jude's dad. He says it is, playing with her. They give him a chair. He cuts the smiling man's hair.

"Nice, nice," the black bubble says, puffed up under the barber cloth, the styling cape and neck strip.

The managers like Jude's technique. Then they tell him how they work. They'll rent him a chair. Jude knows he won't come back, not even for a shave. He thanks the bubble-coated old man, flips him a toonie, and gets the hell out of *Hairy's Place*.

When he receives a call to meet Mr. d'Arborio at a barbershop in the city's north end, Jude reluctantly does.

"A little trick I can do with a *blade*," an old barber is saying in *The Classic Barbershop*.

"You wouldn't shit an old man," d'Arborio is saying.

"No shit, not a trace."

"How do you do it?"

"No knives, only a cut throat straight razor," the barber is saying. "Can give a man a close shave with a straight razor."

When Jude walks in and is introduced, the barber asks him about his skill with a razor.

"I'm getting better and better," he says, "cautious at first."

"This is Mastro Fabrizio," Mr. d'Aborio says, "old-time barber. You're going to shave me. He's going to watch. This barbering master-class is on my dime. He'll teach you his secrets."

The barber doesn't like the word "secrets," and two furrows show on his brow.

"I don't know about this," Jude says.

"You'll be compensated and tipped. Handsomely, and who knows, maybe learn a thing or three. And a haircut, scissors only."

Jude sets out his combs and scissors.

"How old do you think Fabrizio is?"

"Hard to say."

"Say," Mr. d'Arborio says, sitting in the barber chair.

"Forty," Jude says, putting a cape on him. "No, I can't say for sure."

"Forty, eh?" Fabrizio says, turning his head away. "Eighty-two."

"He looks like a little boy," says Jude.

"Disciplined, never eats shit. Dedicated, never cheats. Best barber, innocent, caring. He doesn't play cards."

"You do."

"I do, but not you, Fabrizio."

"Too many barbers risk it all, gambling," the old barber says. "It's a craft and a business. Show me what you can do?"

Jude is reminded of one of his uncles, a skilled, untutored barber that used to cut his hair when Jude was a kid; self-taught, he even cuts his own hair. He always thinks of him as gifted, his Uncle Mike.

The barbering master-class begins.

"Barbers today are more than Figaro or any Joe," Fabrizio says. "They are artists, and some can put a portrait on the back of your head for a couple of hundred bucks. But if you're not Edward Scissorhands, you're a barber with skills such as good conversations with clients and great cuts. You want to be a hairdresser of the year, or to the stars, who cares? You got to learn from the best, and the best aren't always doing the talking. How many heads do you have to cut to earn a living, and to become a real barber, a classic barber? Count them."

He points out to the street.

"Cut throat razor master-class," he says.

The grand master barber watches as Jude shaves his "customer" and cuts his hair. He side-coaches him and steps in from time to time. Then steps away, circles around the chair, and sweeps up the hair. He has been doing that since he was four years old.

Just before he disappears, the master barber grabs Jude's right ear and says: "My angel mother used to say that worries and hair, like the poor, are always with us. So cut with confidence. Hair and worries will always come back."

"Not necessarily on the head," the Shoemaker says.

"Cut hair like an ancient priest doing a sacrifice."

"You're shitting him now, Fabrizio. He wants to be a barber, not a priest. What's this about sacrifice?"

"He understands me."

"Do you? Do you know what the fuck he's talking about?"

"I think I do. It's ceremonial," Jude says, tugging at his earlobe, where the old man has nicked him with his long fingernail, marking him. "It's more than an art."

"It's serious, religious. And don't forget the poor."

"I won't."

"Always be cutting," Fabrizio whispers. "Show you care. Give a damn. Care. Be careful where you go. Be careful what you think and say. Be careful what you do."

"He's telling you to pay attention," d'Arborio says, "like in the old days."

"Amaze us," Fabrizio says, and vanishes.

With that, the master class is over. Too bad he can't work for him, but the old barber works alone. He is a solitary craftsman, not lonely, only alone.

"He coaxed me mostly with facial expressions," he tells Marta later. "He kept moving slowly around me. He was carrying his talent like a sacred gift. No secret revealed, but that there is a secret for you to find in yourself."

"Did you get anything out of it?" she asks.

Jude wants to tell her that this going towards the future feels like escaping into the past. Instead, he says:

"I gave d'Arborio a great cut, just to please, not him, but Mastro Fabrizio. Shaved him with a straight razor."

"And he let you?" Marta asks.

"Also let me put a portrait on the back of his huge head."

"You didn't."

"I did, a subtle but wild image of him as a Joker."

"He paid, d'Arborio?"

"He paid, but I think he snaked me on the tip."

2. THE FALCON SWOOPS DOWN ON BLOOR WEST VILLAGE

The way he tells it later at the Café when they meet to discuss what they have seen and done is that he and Simone have already swooped down on Bloor West Village to check out the barbershops, maybe get a lead on a place for Jude, if he ever leaves his dream of Little Italy.

"So when we slip into Demone's Barbershop, this maniac is yelling and threatening to cut the customer's throat. I thought he was joking, doing the mad barber routine."

"Sweeney Todd," says Simone, "the Demon Barber of Fleet Street."

"Sweeney *whatever*," the Falcon goes on, "demon for sure, demon barber of Bloor West Village. He starts to point the straight razor in my direction, yelling: 'Sit down, sit down, no women, no goddamn women, you need a haircut for sure, long-hair, what the hell, what are you a savage?' 'Are you screaming at me? Are you screaming at me in front of my little lady? What the hell are you yelling about?' He said he wasn't yelling. It was his goddamn shop and he could say what he wanted and do what he bloody well pleased. It seems the guy in the chair wasn't a customer at all, but some other miserable barber he insisted on shaving, nearly cut his head off, cutting his throat. He was showing him the proper technique for a shave. 'Nobody knows how to do it anymore,' he said, and told me to take a chair, got the other guy the hell off the seat. I told him I was there for business, not pleasure. 'What kind of business?' he wanted to know. He didn't do that sort of business (whatever it was) anymore. 'Gave it up,' he said. 'Maybe, if I was talking homemade wine, but even that not so much anymore.' He said if I was talking dope, get the fuck out of his shop."

"'Get behind me, Satan,' is what he said," Simone says.

"He said I looked like Satan, the long hair, the horns on the head. I said they were shades, my sunglasses on my forehead, and could he see straight. He said he'd been losing his eyesight. Drawing blood more and more from poor vision. 'Poor nothing,' I said. 'Maybe, you should stop cutting hair and shaving your victims and trying to kill your clients.' Anyway, I got down to it, asked if he was selling the shop. He asked me who was asking. I told him. He said even if he was I couldn't afford it, and threw out at least a couple of million. Simone said, 'Let's get out of here.' I said, 'Thanks.' He screamed: '*Ciao*, come again, but no women. No goddamn women.'"

"Needless to say, we got out of there," Simone says.

"We got the fuck outta there."

The Falcon pulls out a city map and stabs the location of the Demon Barber. He says that they like the district. They have shops, and you can eat lunch at a Ukrainian restaurant. He says it reminds him of a restaurant in Roncesvalles. Has Jude thought of a place like High Park, maybe along Roncesvalles, all the way down to the lake? It is endless, the search, the discussion, stabbing at the possibilities on a city map.

Jude tells him of his time in the Annex with the homeless guy in the black bubble coat.

"Isn't that what you really want to do?" Marta asks.

"What?" the Falcon asks. "Be a barber to the homeless?"

Jude guesses so.

"Each to his own," the Falcon says. "So why not follow your bliss?"

"Bliss?"

"Do it, man."

He starts talking up the idea. Is it a joke? The Falcon says:

"You can use my pimped-out van. We can go with you. The girls can drum up business, you know, check things out, hand out cards and flyers, point the way to the barber in the van, man, and wiggle their way back with a client or two. Think of the novelty."

Novelty? It sounds crazy. Jude is laughing at the laugh, joking, and jesting. But the Falcon says he is in earnest.

"They bring coffee, blankets in winter, to the homeless, right? Christians, Jews with the homeless vans bring food, clothes and shit to the street people. Why not clean them up? Offer them a haircut."

They get excited. Jude says it is crazy, though the Falcon has penetrated his dream, his longing to help others, at least, be kind.

"You can't make a living, doing charity," he says.

"Money's no object," the Falcon says. "We'll all toss in."

"I've got money," Elena says. "You've got a stake, if what I hear is true."

"I'm in," Marta says. "It sounds right. It sounds just right for you. Do it."

"I can give you a cheque right now," Simone says.

"No, no, no," says Jude, feeling burdened by his guilt-load. "It's just something that I always thought of doing."

He doesn't get to finish. It is a business meeting, whether he likes it or not. The Falcon is already staking out the regions. They will try for a weekend, say. See the city, and have a blast. Jude will get to cut hair. Better than standing looking at himself in the mirror, seeing a sad likeness of himself, cutting his own hair. Better than moaning about the way things are, and always have been. They will get to help a friend. See what comes of it. Let it happen.

"Let's go."

"When?"

"How about right now?"

They are messing around, Jude thinks, trying to keep his spirits up, while he searches for a new shop, before getting it together. It will happen soon enough. The Falcon dashes out to get the van. Elena, Marta and Simone buzz with the excitement of it, doing something together, and doing something nice for Jude.

The Falcon sends Simone a text. He says he is waiting on College in front of the Café. They rush out, Jude lagging behind. They pile in. The Falcon cranks up the tunes. He is playing Drake. The van goes down Clinton for a look. They cheer when they drive past the abandoned shop, *The Lonely Barber*, still picturesque, though shut tight and dark. The Falcon does a U-turn and flies up to College, turns right and speeds off towards Bathurst. He travels southbound to Queen, turns left and sets his sights on the corner of Queen and Sherbourne.

They still call it Skid Row, a downtown slum, but in sight of million-dollar high-rises, and the trendiest of trendy shops. People are playing chess in the park, Moss Park, not far from the homeless shelters, including the Good Shepherd, and St. Paul's Church with the bronze Pietà. On any night, scores of homeless men and women trek to the corner.

"Don't walk down those alleys," the Falcon is saying. "Promise me, you'll never come down here alone, Simone. No joke."

"Sometimes, you gotta walk alone," Simone says.

"Prostitutes walk alone," he says, "and dealers, thieves, drunks, addicts, guys spoiling for a fight."

"The cops don't," Jude says. "They never walk alone down here. They pair up."

"Man, the area has an arena, a ball diamond, lights lighting up the night, boutiques."

"You think you're in Yorkville?"

"Crack is crack, anywhere it's sold. And a mugging is a mugging anywhere it happens, and it can happen anywhere."

"They're robbing you now, just waiting for a streetcar."

"Luxury down here, too. What's safe anymore, anyway?"

"The crazies aren't the problem. They're just sick."

"Man, is that a limo parked out front of a convenience store?"

"Where should I park?" the Falcon asks. "Maybe, nowhere. Maybe back on College. Just circle around, till Jude gets to do what he does. Bums everywhere, man. Hope you brought your Lice Bomb - you're gonna need payload on payload."

"Come on," Jude says.

"Okay, Okay," the Falcon says. "I'm trying, all right? I'm getting better; the poor, the poor are always poor, right?"

"It's what he wants to do," Elena says.

"So, go, don't let me stop you in your work," says the Falcon. "Whoops, there's a cruiser. Are we feeling safe yet?"

"Stop here," Jude says.

They pile out, feeling lost, away from home. Jude walks into the park. Elena, Simone, and Marta stick close. Some of the chess players look over, and some keep their heads down. It isn't going to be easy. Everybody they ask says no. What is their game? Is this a publicity stunt? Are they here to kill the poor, the homeless? Jude leads them to the shelter. He goes in, asks to see somebody in charge, trying to determine if he can help them out by offering free haircuts.

"No, not here, they want food, drinks, coffee, stew and buns. Sweet idea, though, thanks, brother."

Jude tries the church. There is a Mass on. He sits waiting on the steps outside. Does he really want to talk to a priest? He can do that in Little Italy at St. Agnes, or St. Francis of Assisi. Elena says that they should be going. Simone calls the Falcon. He is still circling the park. He pulls up in front of St. Paul's, unlocks the doors, and lets them in. There is total silence until the Falcon breaks it.

"We needed a better business plan," he says.

Jude starts laughing.

"You laugh," the Falcon says, "you laugh. But locked in the van, I never thought I'd ever see you again."

"I'll give it a try by myself," Jude says, "another time."

"Since we're down here, already" says Marta, "why don't we go to the Beaches, down to the Boardwalk, and hang out by the lake?"

They drive to the Beaches, park on Waverley at Queen, and walk down the street to the lake. The Falcon immediately takes off his shirt, sunning himself. Elena and Simone walk down to the water's edge. Marta and Jude sit on a bench and look at the lake. You can see the C.N. tower, looking right, sailboats out in front. Rollerbladers and skateboarders, dogs and their walkers, cyclists, swimmers, people in bikinis playing beach volleyball, kids jumping into the swimming pool, tennis in the tennis courts, Frisbees flying, swooping in arcs all around them.

"I guess, we got spooked," Marta says.

"Nobody spooked us," Jude says. "We just cut and run. I'll go back with a better business plan."

"You got to love our enthusiasm," she says.

"I do," Jude says. "Everybody is just trying to be kind. But as my dad used to say, quoting somebody or other, you need kindness, but you also need facts."

She puts her arm around him, starts in right away massaging his shoulders and neck. He loves her kind of compassion. You can feel it in her touch. So he has to tell Elena that he can't hook up with her, no matter what, and that he just can't stay with somebody he doesn't want to be with. It has to do with love, a memory of that feeling. He has found somebody that he wants to be with. She is sitting with him now, close and getting closer with every breath they take. They are watching the sun go down. The sunset shows how beautiful the place is, the lake and the city in the distance. The others gravitate to the bench.

"Scooch over," the Falcon says.

Elena sits next to Jude. She asks him if he wants a lick of the ice cream she and Simone have bought at the kiosk. Jude takes a quick lick. Elena offers Marta a lick. She takes a couple of licks and passes it back, Jude doing the passing. The Falcon is already licking Simone's. They sit close together in the twilight. They can hear music coming from down at the Boardwalk Café.

"Let's go for an expensive burger," the Falcon says.

"I'm a little peckish," says Simone.

"See you later for the pecking order," he says. "Peckish? I'm famished."

They stride down to the Café, packed with patrons, wait in line, get a table, have shared burgers, except for the Falcon who orders two for himself. He wolfs them down, no problem.

They drive back along Queen. The names of the shops catch their attention. They all love *The Tango Palace*, not a dancehall, but a coffee shop, great name.

"Anyone want a coffee?"

"Not tonight, another time."

It is getting late. A little farther along, Jude happens to glance out the window. That is when he sees it: *The Barber of Leslieville*. He's heard about it.

"Stop," he says.

The window is rolled down. He looks at the shop.

"*The Barber of Leslieville*," says Simone. "I don't know why I didn't say it before. I know the owner."

"Yeah? Who?"

"She might remember me, a woman barber and owner of the shop, Edyta."

"Great name," the Falcon says. "Wonder, do I know her? Maybe, I should."

"At this point, we don't know," Simone says. "I'm the only Polish (or half-Polish) girl you've ever dated, you were saying."

"Maybe, a slight exaggeration, *but*," the Falcon says.

"Interested, Jude?" Marta asks.

"If she's hiring, I need the job. I'm losing my skills. Don't want to go back to supply teaching, or working at the theatre. Is there a number?"

They drive on. Simone looks up the shop on her Blackberry. The website, the blog, the tweets. Jude checks it out. The photos they post show the interior with antlers on the walls; an active shop with women barbers, and guys are drinking beer. Great logo. The shop's website says, yes, she is looking for a barber. Should he go for it? Elena says it is a great idea. The rest are enthusiastic. Send an email. Marta offers to help Jude write it. Simone says she can make a call.

"Besides," the Falcon says, "it is close enough to Skid Row, who knows, if it doesn't pan out, you can go back to Moss Park, and cut hair for the homeless."

3. Elena's Place

Elena invites them all over to her place. She wants to keep the "victory party" going, as she says. They can spend the night. Nobody says anything. The Falcon doesn't want to disappoint her, but. Simone says that maybe it is a little late. They can do it another time. Marta says she will stay, if the others do. Jude says he has to send the email, and won't be much fun, they know how intense he can be, it won't be much of a party, watching a guy on his cellphone, getting the message just right, checking spelling.

Elena is pleading.

"Hey, hey, no tears, not good for you, we've had fun," the Falcon says. "Let's not spoil it."

Marta hands her a Kleenex.

"Let's take you home," she says.

"Why not come up for a bit?" Elena says.

"Sure," Simone says. "Nobody wants to be alone, right?"

"If you're asking," the Falcon says, "I'm coming up, but let me make the snacks and the nightcaps."

Jude gives in, goes along. What else can he do? Elena lives close to the Café. Jude knows her place. He has lived there all those months, not knowing what to do or where to turn. Naturally, he doesn't think anything will come of it. He has liked her. She can be nice. Then when push comes to shove, as it inevitably does, she starts getting pushy, suffocating him. She is prepared for a lot more than he is. It is so easy for expectations to crash-land.

They all go upstairs. The Falcon gets the party started. He bashes into the kitchen, makes up a tray of whatever he finds: Italian bread, cheese, olives, artichokes, salami, and wine.

"Miracle of the Loaves and Fishes," he says, victoriously.

Elena says she doesn't always know what she has in her little kitchen. She tries to make everybody comfortable. She says to Jude to do what he has to do, no problem. She'll keep the music low. The others will eat and drink, listen to music, and talk, maybe a little dancing, so long as nobody has to be alone that night.

Jude smiles at her. The place looks bigger than he remembers it. It is a great place. She even has a section of a church pew for furniture. Expensive furnishings mix with castoffs, found stuff. He likes the couch. It is shaped like large lips, bright red. He sinks into it and starts working on the email. Marta hovers over him, making suggestions when he looks up.

The Falcon moves the tray, the plates, the glasses, in the air, up and over their heads, and down for them to make their choices. He sets everything out. He even lights the candles. Simone is already dancing to the music, Italian love songs from the Sixties.

"I'll be there in a minute," the Falcon says. "Don't start anything meaningful without me, unless you don't mind me watching. It's body-to-body time. I got the time, and whoa, you got the body."

Elena is taking sips of wine, eating a bite of bread, a little piece of cheese, nibbling on an olive. She is smiling hard, looking over at Jude and Marta from time to time. Then she looks up at her other guests. The place can be lonely and often makes her feel lonesome. She likes it with others there. She has missed Jude for so long.

Rita Pavone, the cute, androgynous singer from the early 1960s, is singing "Cuore." The Falcon with arms outstretched lands on Simone, encircles her, sweeps close, and embraces her in a tight hold. They sway and dance. Then arms reach out, as the dancers swing over to Elena, put snaking arms around her, and bring her into the intimate dance. The Falcon is singing into her face. Simone kisses her on the cheek. Elena dances and sings along, until she starts crying.

"No tears," Simone says. "It's just how it is."

"I was so afraid of losing him," Elena says, "that I actually scared him off. We started as lovers and ended as enemies."

"We started as enemies," Simone says, "and I hope you know I'm a friend. It's best that way, being friends, I mean."

"For him, too," says the Falcon.

Jude is enthralled now by the possibility of working for the Leslieville shop. He'll be the Barber of Leslieville. That part of the city creeps into him. He feels it inside his mind and body.

"Let the Lonely Barber stay in his loneliness," Simone says, holding Elena against her.

"He doesn't love me," she says. "Nobody does."

"I love you, El," the Falcon says. "I'm in love with you, too, but it's not the kind of love you like. You're beautiful. You're tiny. You're *a Saturday-Night Special*, small but lethal. You're Miss Firepower of Little

Italy. I'm not afraid of much, but I'm afraid of you."

"He won't speak to me, or if he does, his every word will hurt me," Elena says.

"Words," the Falcon says, "words can hurt, for sure, we all know that. A word can knife you and cut you down. Like Mohammad Ali saying *timber* again and again to intimidate Wilt the Stilt Chamberlain, even though he had slept with a couple of thousand women, he'd never fought a champ, and by hearing the word timber, he was out of the match. Words, words can get inside your head, for sure."

"Are you going to be okay?" Simone wants to know.

"No."

"Come on," the Falcon nudges her. "We'll stay with you. You can sleep between us."

"You don't lose yourself for some guy," Simone says.

"Don't eat your heart out," the Falcon says.

"No," Elena says, "because he'd rather die than let me love him. He'd rather leave than love me."

"It all comes round," the Falcon whispers, and catches a glimpse of himself in the mirror.

"People say I'm jealous," Elena says.

"You are," the Falcon says. "You're even jealous of your own jealousy."

"But nobody is jealous of me," she says. "I always forgive him first, afraid he'll leave me for good. And despite all that's happened, happening, or supposed to, I keep thinking about my sister and what loving somebody did to her."

"I didn't know you have a sister."

"Had," Elena whispers.

"She's not here anymore?"

"She's gone. Adriana's gone."

"Where'd she go?"

"Away. She isn't coming back. She killed herself for some guy."

"Don't let it run in the family," the Falcon says. "Promise me, El."

And despite all that is happening or is supposed to happen (or because of the events of the past summer), Elena talks about her sister. It is the feeling of rejection that brings her dead sister to mind and arrests it, looking over at Lonely and Marta, and takes over her thoughts. Elena believes everybody rejects her; everybody she reaches out to, loves or tries to. Before Lonely, there's one of her grandfather's "associates." She likes to refer to him simply as "D." That is a failing grade she gives him as a lover and human being. She has even slept with him for old times sake when she is seeing Lonely, another mistake, another form of rejection. She always has it in mind that her parents have rejected her. Other members of the family, too, including the ultimate rejection she experiences in losing her sister, Adriana. The loss is violent; too great.

"Death is the ultimate violence," the Falcon says. "I've always thought that the real horror in life is losing a loved one. I don't want to lose anybody."

"She must have stared at the Toronto sunset, and then did it," Elena says. "There was no happiness for her, just as there never will be for me."

"That's too much," the Falcon says. "Too many tears, not enough laughs. Listen, you'll be happy one day, if I can help it."

"I don't need your help, or anybody's," Elena says. "I'm alone. He doesn't want me, or the kid."

Simone won't let her finish. She touches Elena's belly.

"Is there a baby?" she asks, and then holds her close.

"What do you think?"

"What do I think?" the Falcon asks. "No baby, El. There's no baby."

"There is," she says. "I didn't lose it in the hospital. You won't tell about every gory detail, right?"

"We won't tell," Simone says. "But somebody's got to tell."

"And we won't tell lies," the Falcon says. "You got to tell him sometime, and talk it over. We'll just take care of you and the baby, take care of each other."

"The baby's fine," El says. "I'm not."

"Just a hunch," Simone says. "It's not Jude's, is it?"

"No," El says, feeling defeated. "I wanted it to be his."

"Whoa, now, you gotta tell him for sure," says the Falcon.

"I know."

"Who's the father?"

"Never mind."

"Come on, El? Who?"

"Who? Duncan, that's who," she says, trying not to cry.

"That bandit, your grandfather's flunkey? His goon?"

"Him," Elena says.

"Keep the baby, or don't, with or without him," the Falcon says.

"Tell him or don't," Simone says, steering away from any other mention of Duncan.

"I will."

"But you have to tell Jude."

"I know."

Elena glances over at Jude and Marta, sitting close together, composing the email, working out a business plan, and writing out a dream for two. He is lonely no more.

"I'm crying," Elena says, "and he's sitting there dreaming up a life with somebody else."

"That's how the heart is," the Falcon says, holding her close, swaying to the music. "It suffers."

"Cuore,[18]" the singer is singing about the tick and boom of the suffering heart.

The heart suffers. That's how the past gets in, freighted with pain.

"Poor heart," the Falcon says, crying tears of sadness for Elena, and for himself, Simone, Marta and Jude, he sheds blissful tears. Then he mouths the word *timber* over and over again.

---

18   Sung by Rita Pavone

4. END OF SUMMER IN THE SIX

End of summer, and the Shoemaker, his granddaughter and Duncan are having a powwow, a confab, as Duncan calls it, a business meeting. Discussions get quickly out of hand with threats and allegations. Still, what is needed is a settlement, a decision.

"No police, no police," Elena is screaming.

"Get him, get him," one of the Shoemaker's Shadows shouts, dragging Duncan in pieces back.

"I'm on it," the other one shouts back, sitting Duncan back in his chair.

The Shadows have disarmed Duncan. Elena has taken a knife from her grandfather. Napkins are thrown in to deal with the bleeding and the blood.

"She's your fiancée," the Shoemaker says, "based on what you did, with another guy taking the blame, mistaken twice."

"Fiancée, my ass," Duncan says. "She's still in love with that barber."

"Is that any way to talk to your fiancée?" the Shoemaker asks.

"Talk, my ass," Duncan says, cleaning blood from his nose. His nostril has been nicked. "I'll show you fiancée."

He reaches into his inside jacket pocket and pulls out photos, and throws them into their midst like confetti. There is a mad scramble for the pics.

"Give me those goddamn photos."

"What is this?"

"I've been tracking her for months."

"You were tracking Simone," Elena says.

"Same *dif*," he says. "Caught you both, and with the same fucking guy."

"That's over," the old man says. "Get every photo. Not one of them gets out of here alive."

The pictures show Jude with Elena, and Simone with Jude, then Elena with Jude in a Fiat 500 Pop. The story is that Duncan has pursued them, not because he is working for anybody, but because he is insanely jealous. Elena hugs him around the waist and keeps calling him an asshole.

"I guess you love me," she says, "in your own stupid asshole way."

"Love?" the old man says. "Yours is no "*Al-di-là*"[19] romance."

"He's jealous of me," she says. "Somebody has to be, *beyond the beyond*. As well him as anybody else."

"I'll apologize or sign a peace bond, but it's not an admission of guilt," Duncan blurts out, as if in a court of law.

A settlement is arrived at. Love or no love, jealousy or no jealousy, the match is made in hell, as the Shoemaker says.

"You deserve each other."

An EMS vehicle arrives. Duncan is put in the back. He has sustained multiple wounds, threatening or non-life-threatening. At that point, they don't know. Later, they do.

---

19   Beyond the beyond

5. LONG GONE

End of summer, in the city heat of one Toronto summer in the span of two months, the matter has been concluded. It has also been settled for Jude. He has lost what he has taken time to build. One summer, in the Toronto summer of 2014, he finds himself a new identity, Lonely no more, but Jude, the Barber. He has lost his shop, which never opened, yet has found love and work elsewhere.

These are the things, counter and strange, that Simone is saying to Jude when they meet in private to hash it out and finish their date, long overdue now from before the kidnapping, interrogation, release, flight from, and return to, the city.

"Long gone," he says, "long gone, and never coming home."

But is it long gone? Love? The past? Isn't he coming home? Sometimes, Jude is fearful, by his own admission, though usually unstated or understated in conversations with family or friends. He keeps saying he is afraid of it. Yet full of longing to be able to defy the past or lost love, and ramble on.

"I mean, the past doesn't exist," he says to Simone, once they get a chance to reflect on the past and on what might have been.

What about love?

"Neither does the future," is how she puts it, pointing to the only alternative.

Now, now, now, only the present can be counted on or even counted. But it has to be endured. It trips to stumble and rattles like windows against the wind. For him, this place and every place he has ever been to and has ever seen and abandoned is filled with stormy draughts of desolate wind. He hears the wind, tiptoeing across a dark room, or walking on the balls of his feet across the street. Time is a kind of pit, swallowing the curiosity of all adventurers like him. He is standing where echoes define the emptiness. That is when he whispers his lover's name, but there is definitely no echo.

"Besides the emptiness we all feel sometimes, besides the deals we make with those who promise and promise happiness, they con me into hope."

When he sleeps alone, his room is a loud, pounding drum, or the thumping of keys on a tortured, spray-painted upright piano sitting in a public space, say, outside Koerner Hall. Or it is as tender as pain that has gone after a long sleep. He tells Simone that her absence and this gesture of saying goodbye will leave their marks on him. From now on, she can find him gawking through windows at mirrors in a barbershop.

She tells him that at one time with stones in her throat, she spoke in no uncertain terms about life and of what sense she made out of it, of losses, of panic in states of rage, her clinical ways of grasping at virtue now that she looks beyond his blistered hooded eyes.

The air is thick from heavy breathing. It is passed on through bruised lips like the blue-veined pulse of the blues.

"I dress for every situation," Simone says. "I was dressed for you. You never really had a chance to see me naked."

"My eyes were closed," he says.

It begins with kindness and seems kind of tragic for them. They are both going nowhere, but thinking otherwise. It has seemed to them that it can be cured by love. So they head in that direction. They want to love with a deep and mad love. Love is too loaded a word for what they want to have.

"I wanted to love you," he says. "I was aiming to, spoiling to, and all set."

"I wanted you to," she says.

When Lonely thinks about love, he can't help wanting to penetrate its madness.

"Seemed to me you needed love," he says.

"So you tried to love, but not *me*," she says.

"I wanted to love you, memorize your voice, your cry, your moan, and interpret the shadows and contours, the moonbeams on your body."

He doesn't say this. He is still left with the impression that he and Simone are trying to ride that tragic kindness of love that never has a chance.

"I loved and loved and loved," he wants to say when love ends, "but it never got started."

He is feeling reckless, as if mouthing her name, *Simone*, can spell out another go at it. Like a fit of longing, it convulses them.

"You played in the wreckage like a kid in a junkyard," she wants to say, but doesn't, "too far off in wonder-joy to bother about scraped knees, bruised elbows, broken bones or stitches to the head to watch your footing over your amazement at love."

"Like sewing machines, record players, rocking chairs," he wants to say, but can't.

"Like things thrown out," she wants to say, but doesn't, "you knew me as a discarded daughter, a lover of wooden dolls, woollen cats, and world music abandoned in childhood, and damned to curse the brutal beauty of squalor as I grew up."

Neither one speaks for a while. Simone recalls countless boyfriends, and midnight sleepwalking for drugs ready for her tongue. Gazes fixed, they search for artefacts, evidence, and proof of love. Is any of this really happening?

"I can picture you," he says, "when we first met. You were almost smiling, squinting. Your face marked from the wrinkles that your smile left."

But she is thinking that he can't picture her, not as she really is.

"I welcome at least your surveying touch."

She does not say this. Nor does she tell him what is different about her now at the end of summer. She doesn't tell him all she feels for the Falcon. That information is classified. They try to talk about what happened on their interrupted lunch date: the fear of missing out, the idea of love, the ice cream, the beating, and escape. But the past flips them the bird.

He wants to say to her, but doesn't: "We just never got it right."

And he reminds her about Elena's jealousy and his own feelings. Simone says that nobody can afford a full breakdown right now. She has really surprised herself the way she has pushed the words out so that they might drown her.

New opportunities arrive silent as the ones before to say what they can't say, and things they would have said, if their affair had taken place. What might have been. He would have told her about his visits to the Vespa shop, and watching Italian films, *Cinema Paradiso* and *The Bicycle Thief* and *La Dolce Vita*.

She knows he sees himself in *The Bicycle Thief*, and sees himself in the masklike face of his grandfather in the picture he carries in his wallet.

There is so much to say, but they never have a chance to. His thoughts are running scared, running wild. Those quiet thoughts that she dares not speak, secrets she has learned when young, a family's open secrets with talking wounds not allowed to talk. The accusations will come if they stay together.

"The closer I am to your broken heart," he wants to say, but doesn't, "the closer I am to you."

"We couldn't get close," she is on the point of saying, but can't find the words to say it.

"I know you dance alone," he wants to say. "Meet me after hours at the café or by the dancehall parking lot and we'll have a talk to end all talks, as if that would ever happen."

They are walking in the old neighbourhood, eating an ice cream—they find lemon gelato—Simone's treat. It is the speed that has surprised them both, the thrift of events, the economy of intentions, people and purposes mistaken and mistook. But not forsaken, they love other people now. He has called her sweet angel. Once. And once, they date on the brink of new love, a summer fling, a Toronto romance.

"We never had a chance," she says.

"Chance had everything to do with the brain dance," he says, "and with us."

How the story tells itself, how the plot thickens in the revenge game battle with the Shoemaker. It is all about survival. How he claims he has won her, his sweet angel. She says she hopes they can be friends without fringe benefits. She won't ever want to hurt the Falcon, her sweet angel, her new love, and if it works out, more than just her man.

Jude has his Marta, his city girl, urban chic with all she can be, preferring the city to its absence. She doesn't want them to miss out on what the city has to offer, from its neighbourhoods to its tower, its parks and islands.

Simone and Jude talk it over and realize that by the end of summer they have become fast friends without even trying. Both have been abducted, interrogated and released. They have won by not trying to win. They kiss and part.

"What did you say to each other?" the Falcon asks, picking up Simone.

"We said this, that," Simone says, "and all that we never got to say to each other, and would never get to say, because it ended before it began. We didn't say what we would have said."

"You okay?" the Falcon asks, leaning in for a kiss.

"I'm okay," she says, and kisses him hard.

"Better than just okay," he says. "You're miraculous."

When she sits next to him, the Falcon swoops down on her with a diamond-hard question. But she lunges at him with a real diamond. She asks him first. She wants to propose to him before he has a chance to propose to her.

6. Wedding at Grace & Dundas

The ceremony is to take place at St. Francis of Assisi with Reception to follow in the St. Agnes Church Basement.

When it happens, it happens fast. It happens all at once, or it doesn't. Some believe they're going to hell in a hand basket, while some boyfriend or spouse or louse is trying to live a dream. Some believe in closure, while others remain inconsolable, bogged in sorrow. Everybody needs somebody to blame until you own your pain and the hurt you cause yourself and others. It happens quickly. What stays? What fades out? What dies? What is reborn?

When the party at Elena's breaks up around 4 in the morning, the Falcon goes home with Simone. They have stayed long enough, but they can take it. They too are making plans, ever since their trip to the end of the world, not the Shwa, but you could see it from there, another home is their destination, their own. Jude thanks Elena for understanding. He has been hunched over the cellphone, getting his message right. She has a moment with him later in the kitchen, while Marta is in the washroom, and she tells him what has really happened. She tells Jude:

"No baby for us. There's a baby, but it's not yours. You're free, free of me."

They don't say anything else to each other. They are just sad, but free.

"It was just too sad," Jude tells Marta later.

When they leave, they leave Elena alone. When it happens, it happens all of a sudden. Or not. Synchronicity, too, happens. Everything happens at the same time, despite the reason. It slides, collides, coalesces, and breaks apart. It begins again. Is that why everything happens for a reason, especially grief? The universe may be dying, as they can prove, but Jude hears back from the shop in Leslieville. Sure, the owner, Edyta, will give him a tryout, a chance, she is open to it, and wants to see what he can do. She explains how she works, and her dream for the shop. Her dream is hard work, but relaxed. She has been resilient. She has to be because she is in business for herself. Though it is a male-dominated business, she will succeed. Jude can come and go as he pleases, but they are busy for the time being. The shop is popular. Jude can work, get out of debt, and start a new life. In time, build his own shop, on his own, his own way. When he tells his new employer, she likes his story about the Lonely Barber, and the buzz it has created, like an urban legend, and the collective variations on the story. It is easy for him to work for a female boss. The Falcon, when he is told about it, says:

"Right on. That's how it should be. We *be* how it should be. That's how it is, working for women."

The boss agrees to store Jude's barber chair. He begins working right away. It is time to get behind his dummy for real. The days are long. From the first day on the job in the Leslieville shop, Jude hits it off with the other barbers; tattoos and piercings, Irish-born, or from Australia. Edyta is as smart as she is passionate. The shop is hot and hopping with plenty of heads to get to know. Haircuts, beer, talk, and tips, unless they try to short-change you. How many heads does he have to know to be able to make a living? That recurring question gives it a business sense. A simplified life has a cost, but can Jude survive, thrive, and stay alive? More than subsistence wages, more than paying bills, can he make it?

"Scissors and hair," he says.

Not every barber gets a place in Florida. The wealthy barber, is it fact or fantasy?

"It's a business," the old barber, Fabrizio, has already told him.

Up flash all the struggles of the past: the part-time jobs, the classes, the missed opportunities, mix-ups and missteps, even minor successes and big flops, gambles and sure things. They are finished with; gone. It has happened. Jude is a pro.

Another thing happens. Jude takes the streetcar one day after work to Moss Park. He plays chess, offers his opponent a coffee from his thermos, espresso. The guy offers him a flask: cheap whiskey. They drink and play. Jude ends up giving him a haircut. He has his kit with him in a black rucksack. The other chess players and drifters see what's going on. So it begins. It happens in Skid Row. Whenever he can, he is the Lonely Barber for the homeless. At work, he is a professional barber, improving his skills, getting better and better, especially with the fade: the Barber of Leslieville. He even starts helping people, connecting one client with another, a kind of modern-day barber-surgeon, as if dealing with the bloodletting and suggesting cures for city-dwellers. One day, a hip, developmentally prepubescent boy comes into the shop for a trim, and keeps chanting, "Come on, blow on it, buddy, blow on it." And Jude blows on his comb and blows hard on the back of the boy's neck, and the young hipster is wildly happy, wriggling and giggling in the barber chair.

Then Jude and Marta talk about getting married. After all, wedding plans are in the air, especially in Little Italy. Simone has proposed to the Falcon. He has accepted, crying like a baby. Simone has spent time in detox. She credits the Falcon for getting her off prescription drugs in his campaign to get her to avoid the opioids, as he says. He insists that food, drink and love are the best habits for humans. He promises to cook for her and fill her glass with wine, and love her as if their love is written in the stars, the greatest lovers in Little Italy, no pre-nup agreement necessary, just trust. They even have a picture taken at the corner of College and Grace, sitting with the bronze statue of Johnny Lombardi.

At the Falcon and Simone's wedding, Elena is the Maid of Honour. Jude is the best man. With the sudden *kindness* and council of the Shoemaker and Duncan's legwork, though he limps from a good beating, they are able to get St. Francis of Assisi Church for the wedding, and the St. Agnes Church Hall for the reception. It has to be catered. No sweat. The Falcon will do most, if not all, the cooking. Friends from the Café Del Popolo pitch in. Simone gets a man who can cook, a man who worships the ground beneath her feet, and breathes in every ounce of musk oozing out of her pores. He says so at the reception.

It comes out when the couple makes their sweet vows at the altar that the Falcon's first name is Dion. His father has named him for the doo-wop singer from the nineteen-fifties, Dion Di Mucci, of Dion and the Belmonts fame, saying his son should always put the bop in the shoo-bop and the wop in the doo-wop in anything he does in life, and the Falcon yelps and cries out with a war whoop, as if he has just been born: "Dion, the Falcon, Falconieri." He will hear about it in the streets, his secret name revealed, but eventually they will go back to calling him the Falcon, as he wishes, except maybe for Simone who has permission to call out his true name in the name of love and in the moan of passion on their honeymoon.

Jude and Marta talk about getting married when they go for a walk to get some air from dancing up a sweat in the hot church basement and eating too much Italian and Polish food. He says he is putting on a few, but has to stay lean for his work. They stroll behind the church and up to Clinton. When they get to the abandoned barbershop, the site of *The Lonely Barber*, with no trace of the sign anymore and no lights on, Jude says it is a good idea for them to get together. They stroll back to the reception, holding each other tight.

Then join the other guests still parading and streaming into the church hall (the basement). The place is festooned with crepe paper streamers and decorated with lilacs, daisies (Simone's favourites) and yellow and white roses (the Falcon's preferred flowers). The wedding cake is in the shape of a vintage red Fleetwood Cadillac with long fins, instead of a gondola, which is second choice. The band is still playing wedding tunes. More drinks are poured. Wine and beer flow from the open bar. A sweets table is rolled in, laden with liqueurs, Italian and Polish pastries, almond cookies and assorted biscotti. Food comes out of the kitchen in courses, some of it flaming. No Quail, even though the Falcon likes devouring them, Simone can't stomach eating little birds.

Elena is dancing with Duncan, towering over her, under the watchful eyes of her grandfather and his deep purple Shadows. Both Elena's parents aren't there. Her father can't make the trip, even when he knows about the wedding, and her mother is in Montreal chasing after some guy named Arturo, a musician, and can't be contacted. According to her grandfather, their absence is to blame for the succession of events that have led to Duncan and then Jude and back to Duncan again. Now, Elena and Duncan are doing a tarantella, sort of, because Duncan doesn't know how, but can pretend. It is tough to dance with a crutch, so he is using a cane.

The Shoemaker, wearing his electric blue suit, with points of light shooting off the fabric, an immaculate white shirt and a saffron tie, and the shiniest shoes anyone has ever seen, is prevailed upon to sing (or he has insisted on singing and has insinuated himself) a song of his choosing, and he takes the microphone away from the band leader and sings a *stornello amoroso* in honour of the newlyweds, and dedicates the same song as well to his granddaughter and her new fiancé. Jude can hardly believe the beauty of the old man's voice. It is like listening to a killer singing an aria in a *Bel Canto* tenor. Some say the old man sounds like Domenico Modugno, but others compare him to Claudio Villa from the past. The Shoemaker can sing to make you cry and break your heart. Even the Shadows are moved.

Jude tells Marta that in the song the lover's destiny is written in the heart of the beloved. Even if life is poisonous, he wants to be with her always. For her mouth, red-lipped and perfumed, he will gladly lose his life. He will die just to be able to tell the world that he has kissed her. If she were a queen and he a king, he would lavish her with pearls from the Orient in exchange for her fascinating love.

Jude now sees the singer in a different light. The old man singing gives him a glimpse into his past, his youth, striving to make it in the city. He must have been in love once. He must have worked hard to get by. Of course, like the rest of them in the neighbourhood, and what the Italians had been through. With immigration, bigotry, prejudice, knife fights, especially with stilettos as reported in the press, the murder victims of the Black Hand, and unemployment, it had been a struggle to survive. The Shoemaker is the old guard in Little Italy, but won't let go. He has made a living, gained social status and ground and political influence. He can still take on all comers and contenders.

Despite two black eyes (shiners covered up by shades), and pain in his knees from a thorough going-over prior to his engagement, Duncan is holding Elena tight, dancing, if you can call it that, like a praying mantis with a tiny insect. He holds her in the clinch. He keeps drinking shots and proposes toasts to the Shoemaker and to his unborn child, saying,

"We'll name him Pietro after you. Or Scarpetta, if it's a girl, the little shoe."

The Shoemaker isn't altogether pleased with the number of times a glass or bottle is raised violently in his direction from the dance floor and drunk to his health, especially by Duncan.

With Jude, Duncan begins blurting out a kind of confession of past wrongdoings, crimes and misdemeanours, but with no hard feelings, and thankful that he hasn't called the cops.

"No police," Duncan says, gratefully. "No police."

He keeps saying what a real man Jude is. He also says how Simone has led him into the business in the first place. "Women being women" is his phrase, as he is sure Jude can understand, or will soon find out. For this, he is smacked repeatedly. Elena extends herself on tiptoes and bites into his chin to show him what women are, if he ever says it again.

"No more disrespect," she says.

But Duncan is intent on telling his tales of violence and violation. Every alley has a story. Every café and bar has its incident and event. For local history, he is not its historian, but a player, agent, and participant. The stilettos of the past are nothing in comparison to the arsenal of the present day. Jude's "case" is only one of the scores that Duncan has undertaken to settle, orchestrate and carry out on someone else's behalf.

"I'm not naming names," he says, "but I'll soon be related to him."

These tales are unredeemable, but worth telling. As Duncan speaks, he reaches out his silver-handled walking stick and bops the trumpet player, intentionally or unintentionally, no one can be sure, on the mouth. When he hits the bell straight on with the flat of his other hand, the trumpet player stops playing. His mouth is bleeding. What about his teeth and tongue?

Knives out. Are they stilettos, like those of the past? His, and the bandleader's, and the Shoemaker's and the old man's Shadows all flash. They wield knives, ready for a knife fight, but it resembles a dance.

"This is for you."

"No, this is for you."

"This is for both of you."

The colour red bleeds from their hands. Will faces, chests and guts bleed at this wedding?

"Why am I getting the *asshole* treatment?" Duncan implores, blood spilling from his cut finger.

"Because you're an asshole," the Shoemaker says.

A blood droplet stains the collar of his white shirt. The band members get involved. So do the wedding guests. The priest takes out his cellphone to call 911.

"No police, no police," Elena is screaming. "We've all got records."

"Get him, get him out of here," one of the Shadows says.

"I'm on it," the other one says.

The Falcon has disarmed Duncan. Elena has taken the knife from her grandfather. The priest deals with the band. Napkins are thrown in to deal with the bleeding and the blood such as there is. The knives vanish.

"This is a goddamn wedding," Elena says, "not the World Cup Finals."

Duncan's nostril has been nicked again. She dabs at it with a Kleenex and her own spit. Elena hugs him around the waist and keeps calling him an asshole. Some say she calls him a beautiful asshole, moved by his attempt to save face. He apologizes to the band and pleads with them to play a special piece for the Shoemaker, for old time sake, and to keep the peace. Reluctantly, they do. But the Falcon interrupts the accordion player, playing a mock version of *Rusticana Cavalleria*, and begins doing beat-box and rapping, in dedication to his new bride, Simone, saying she fills him and he fills her with equal power and desire.

The Falcon (Dion Falconeri) tells his wedding guests that his new *do* is courtesy of his one and only barber, Jude, no longer the Lonely Barber, and he gives him a shout-out and recommends him to all the hipsters and oldsters alike, and Jude says, "Cheers" and thanks him with jazz hands in the air.

"The Barber, not of Seville," he says, "but of Leslieville."

"*Ahimè, che folla!*" the Shoemaker sings.

"*Uno alla volta, per carità!*

Ehi, Figaro!

Son qua. Figaro qua, Figaro là,

Figaro su, Figaro giù."[20]

Then the Falcon raps his hip-hop goodbyes, saying it is good to be alive, with a great new haircut, in love, married, with the sweet smell of blood and pastries in the air, and still crazy and true. He swears that madness is a blessing, and that love is sweet madness, and that sex is the sweetest, mad blessing of all. He says that what doesn't kill you, likely kills the guy next to you, but also makes you stronger. Truth be told, a few fear this moment might turn into a twist or variation on the urban legend, "the Vengeful Groom." But though he has been drinking shots, he blesses them with tears in his eyes, saying that one hand washes the other in the matter of one-love, all by blowing kisses and hoping they've enjoyed the meal he has prepared for the wedding feast, especially for his bride, Simone.

Simone throws the bouquet. It arcs over her shoulder, a backward deadly aim, and Elena almost catches it, and when she slips and misses, Marta manages to wrestle it away from grasping hands. She is next. Everybody says so. She says it loudest of all. The newlyweds, the wedding party and the guests parade through the neighbourhood, up past the abandoned barbershop and the Café Del Pop. Cheers rise up from the patio. It is an August night, and on this Toronto summer night, everything is lit up and shining, and the newlyweds are taking

20   From "The Barber of Seville" by Rossini

the Fleetwood Cadillac for a honeymoon in Niagara Falls. The Falcon and Simone kiss everybody on the lips, and the groom helps his bride into the passenger side, ready to fly, and turns to the guests with arms stretched out wide.

"What do you think?" the Falcon asks family and friends, concerning Simone's bridal beauty, as he calls it. "And what do you say? Am I fucking right?"

It is his wedding day, and he is feeling the love and living the miracle of it, heartbeat to heartbeat. So it goes with the Falcon and Simone. What else can the guests say, waving goodbye and good luck, and, happy or unhappy, wishing the bride and groom joy and madness for the remainder of their mortal and immortal lives, but keep going on and on, and never feel defeated, and what else can Jude and Marta say, or Elena for that matter, or even Duncan or Mr. d'Arborio, looking like one of the local dignitaries who numbers among the wedding guests, or even a Queen Bee buzzing around the Italian Rum Balls and other desserts, what else can anybody say, and what else is there to say at the end, but right, fucking right?

7. AFTERWORD: SCISSORS & HAIR

So it goes in the city. So it goes for urban hipsters, crusaders, and urban saints. And so it goes with the Falcon and Simone on their honeymoon at the Falls. So it goes for Elena and Duncan, who have already had their honeymoon, and are expecting a baby. For Jude and Marta, it goes that way, too, which is their own way, and goes on and on in a City Hall wedding. The same place that has rejected Jude's shop approves his civil union. Voices from the city's neighbourhoods, districts and villages babble, palaver, clamour, clash, lift up and coalesce to tell the same story.

The hope is for a new day, a new way, stepping out of yesterday into today. Hoping against hope that the first instant, the first kiss, the first promise, the first step are important on the first day, leading to tomorrow, and that they lead to the next step and on and on. Jude and Marta have an intimate reception at the People's Café, stay the night in Toronto, and then head off to Montreal for a quick honeymoon and straight back to the city for work.

There is plenty of work. At the time, and because of the popularity of the shop, Jude is cutting 80 to 100 heads per week. The shop is prosperous thanks to the ingenuity of the owner, Edtya. The wild boys come in to get her to cut their hair, some just to get a load of the hipster atmosphere, and feel the touch of fingers in their hair, and check themselves out in the mirror. Some come in, because they want to be near her, look like her, or *be* her. Some of the clients love Sylvester, the real pro, with his campy come-ons and jokes about sexuality. The actors, writers, and filmmakers come in to get a professional cut from Larry, covered in tattoos and a real barber. Still others come in on referral from happy customers or walk-ins that see the antlers on the wall and the cans of beer in the hands of barbers and clients alike. A client walks in, takes a chair, and Jude starts up a conversation. No jive, the barber's straight talk impresses the one getting a haircut. Jude realizes he is a barber with an attitude. No, not an attitude, but a past and a view of the past. But he feels he is discarding the past with each snip of the scissors. Hair falls to the floor, and is eventually swept up, like the past.

And Jude will tell his own version of the story of the summer. It is now written down in the third person for distance, but also in their hearts, and many voices tell it over and over again. How he calls it *The Lonely Barber*. It is the name he has given to a little shop situated for a while in Little Italy in that one sweet summer of the past. He is ready to open soon, but the paperwork says otherwise. The glitch is that you can set up a shoemaker shop (it has been approved and zoned for one forever), but not a barbershop. It is a lesson Jude has to learn in business. The business of business is business. But it is also a tale of tenacity, creativity and originality that he tells those select clients that are prepared to hear it, and tell their own stories of city life.

He says that he works hard with his partner, now his wife, to find, design and build a new life. In love and work, he wants to get things right. He only cuts one guy's hair in *The Lonely Barber*, a young man who lives in the neighbourhood, and peeks in to see what the hell is going on. He is so excited about the prospect of a barbershop so close to home that the barber, moved by his enthusiasm, gives him a free haircut and a free espresso. The quest for the shop involves weeks of dreaming and working. Their play and toil capture people's attention and imagination. Some also feel blocked, helpless. Out of that bewilderment and frustration, some feel proud, as the heart sings at the resilience and endurance of the human spirit to dream, love and work.

Is it safe to say that some of the episodes and plot twists and turns never really happen, and that they are made up as the urban romance moves along? The interrogation episode, for instance, is it believable or does it stretch credulity? The double kidnappings: are they pure inventions, made up to express the feelings of intrigue and entanglement with what it is like to fight City Hall? And what about the car chase as a road trip or fantasy with the Karmann Ghia and the Fiat 500 Pop (Jude's father has always wanted a Karmann Ghia and Fiat 500 Pop, maybe not in those colours)? The shop happens, but the timing seems against fact, and therefore closer to fiction. Necessary inventions for the storytelling, good or bad, in the end, they amount to the same thing in the face of roadblocks and setbacks. The tiny miracles that Jude once writes about in one of his stories, he lives out in the way he helps others, loves and dreams. He is the hardest worker anybody knows. He is a teacher, a writer, and now a barber. He is also a son, brother, friend and spouse. His city-born romance moves from violence to cooperation. Everybody is better for knowing him, and he is better for knowing everybody. You don't always get to choose who tells your story, or how it gets told. But the urban tale is a somewhat edgy and belated wedding gift, a dark urban love story for their coming together, despite the odds, and staying true and strong in pursuit of their love-dream. If he ever gets lonely, it's not for lack of company and those that are still crazy about him. So it goes as time and the city fly by. So it goes for Jude, the once Lonely Barber, now *lonely* no more.

ACKNOWLEDGEMENTS

My gratitude goes to my son, Nic,
for his generosity, advice and example.

I would also like to thank Dr. Anna Faktorovich
for her kind acceptance of this work.

OTHER
ANAPHORA LITERARY
PRESS TITLES

PLJ: Interviews with Gene Ambaum and Corban Addison:
VII:3, Fall 2015
Editor: Anna Faktorovich

Architecture of Being
By: Bruce Colbert

The Encyclopedic Philosophy of Michel Serres
By: Keith Moser

Forever Gentleman
By: Roland Colton

Janet Yellen
By: Marie Bussing-Burks

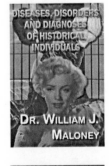

Diseases, Disorders, and Diagnoses of Historical Individuals
By: William J. Maloney

Armageddon at Maidan
By: Vasyl Baziv

Vovochka
By: Alexander J. Motyl

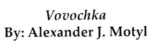

CPSIA information can be obtained
at www.ICGtesting.com
Printed in the USA
LVOW08s0900090717

540729LV00002B/312/P